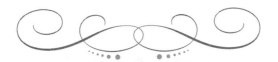

# SIMPLY
# SANE

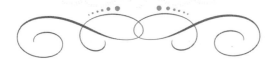

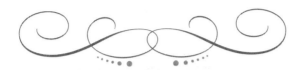

# SIMPLY
# SANE

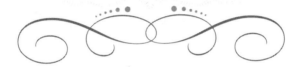

## LIVING OUTSIDE
## THE FAST LANE

DEBBIE BOWEN

**Horizon**
**Springville, Utah**

ISBN 13: 978-0-88290-958-5

Published by Horizon, an imprint of Cedar Fort, Inc., 2373 W. 700 S., Springville, UT 84663
Distributed by Cedar Fort, Inc., www.cedarfort.com

LIBRARY OF CONGRESS CATALOGING-IN-PUBLICATION DATA

Bowen, Debbie, 1962-
  Simply Sane: living outside the fast lane / Debbie Bowen.
    p. cm.
  ISBN 978-0-88290-958-5
  1. Mothers--Psychology. 2. Mothers--Time management. 3. Family--Time management. 4. Stress management for women.  I. Title.

  HQ759.B7534 2009
  640'.43--dc22


  2008043667

Cover design by Nicole Williams
Cover design © 2009 by Lyle Mortimer
Edited and typeset by Melissa J. Caldwell

Printed in the United States of America

10  9  8  7  6  5  4  3  2  1

Printed on acid-free paper

*To everyone recklessly speeding*
*down the fast lane of life . . .*
*pull over, slow down, and enjoy the ride.*

## *Other works by Debbie Bowen*

W.O.R.K.—Wonderful Opportunities for Raising
Responsible Kids

Nobody's Better Than You, Mom!

# Contents

# Not Everything Worth Doing Is Worth Doing Well

Early one morning, a young man was walking down a lonely beach when he saw an old man in the distance throwing something into the sea. As the young man approached, he watched the old man pick up a stranded starfish and throw it into the water. Again and again, the old man kept throwing starfish.

"What are you doing?" asked the young man. The old man explained that the starfish would die if left on the beach under the morning sun.

"But there are thousands here on the beach!" cried the young man. "You can't possibly save all of them—you can't even make a difference!"

The old man looked at the starfish in his hand and then threw it into the safety of the sea. Turning to the young man, he said, "I made a difference to that one."[1]

☆  ☆  ☆

Not everything worth doing is worth doing well, but that doesn't mean it isn't worth doing. While you may not be able to save all the starfish, "a second rate Something is better than a first rate Nothing."[2]

Sometimes "good enough" is good enough.

## You Cannot Be All Things to All People at All Times

In the early years of my marriage, I suffered from "delusions of grandeur." In my overly-ambitious way, I imagined that my house would always be immaculately clean—even the fridge, the oven, *and* the windows; my children would always be neatly dressed in cute little outfits that I had made myself; and I would prepare three nutritious, well-balanced meals every day that included all four food groups. At least once a week I would try some new gourmet recipe, and I would keep my children happy by baking an assortment of delicious desserts.

Well, it didn't take long for reality to hit me! When I woke day . . . after day . . . after day with those terrible feelings of morning sickness or I was carrying a fussy newborn on my hip while trying to fix dinner, I can promise you gourmet was the last thing on my mind.

When my first child was six months old, I decided

it was time to make one of those cute little outfits I had dreamed about. Enthusiastically, I set up my sewing machine, put my sewing basket at the kitchen table, and went to work. However, my little son saw my sewing project as a room full of exciting new play toys. He promptly became preoccupied with pushing the foot pedal to the sewing machine while I tried to sew, scattering pins all over the kitchen floor and creating a tangled mess of unwound bobbins and spools of thread. It did not take long for me to decide that I was not having fun!

I learned early on that sewing with little children around is extremely difficult; consequently, I have not made nearly as many of those cute little outfits as I once imagined. Ten children later, I just feel grateful if my little darlings are dressed in something reasonably clean and mostly free from holes when we leave the house. And I consider it an added bonus if both socks are matching!

My house is not immaculate either. I struggle to keep the kitchen counter from becoming a dumping ground for all those little odds and ends that no one wants to take care of, and I don't think my walls have been smudge-free since that first little baby began leaving fingerprints on them more than twenty years ago. Initially, the smudges were restricted to an area eighteen inches from the floor. Today, with children ranging from small to over six feet tall, I have fingerprints and scuff marks everywhere. Incidentally, I am still trying to figure out how my children's "non-marking soles" leave a trail of scuff marks on all the baseboards and how we came to have a black scuff mark at the *top* of the bathroom door. (When it comes right down to it, I probably don't really want to know.)

There is no doubt about it—I have come a long way since I was first married. In some ways I am a different person than I once thought I would become. I have learned to relax and let go. Over the years, I have learned that some things really don't matter; and I no longer spend precious time or energy worrying about those things.

This new approach to life evolved slowly and has not been achieved without conscious effort and a fair amount of internal distress. It all began years ago as a young mother of a four-year-old, a two-year-old, and a baby. My husband was working to support us while pursuing a doctoral degree. Twice a week, he attended an evening class, arriving home about 10 PM. Because my husband was so busy outside the home, I assumed most of the care of the house, the yard, and our three little children. I pushed myself so hard that I became physically ill. Increasingly overwhelmed and discouraged—single-handedly trying to save every starfish as it were—it became obvious that I had set some unrealistic expectations for myself.

One evening I attended a meeting where the

speaker said something so profound and so liberating that it left a lasting impression. Although I do not remember anything else she said that night, I have never forgotten one statement: "You cannot be all things to all people at all times."

It was as though she was speaking directly to me, and I went home that very night and began implementing that new philosophy in my life. I stopped feeling grief and guilt for all the things I could not do or for not doing them as well as I would have liked. I realized that I could not be the perfect wife, mother, housekeeper, gardener, neighbor, and friend all at the same time. In fact, I could not even be all things to all of my children at the same time. I learned to prioritize my family's needs, focusing on one person at a time, without feeling like I was neglecting the others. Gradually, I learned to slow down, cut back, let go, and go without—and it has made all the difference.

In our rigorous, fast-paced, competitive world, there is incredible pressure to succeed at all costs. Too often success is defined as excellence; and excellence means outsmarting, outpacing, and outdoing the competition. As victims of this be-all, do-all mentality, we have fallen prey to three harmful myths: 1) Supermen and superwomen are real; 2) any job worth doing is worth doing well; and 3) spending time on yourself is a selfish, superficial use of time. Only by recognizing these myths and accepting their false premises can we learn to overcome them. This book will discuss three substitutes for these myths:

- ☆ **Fact 1:** Supermen and superwomen are NOT real.

- ☆ **Fact 2:** Not everything worth doing is worth doing well.

- ☆ **Fact 3:** Making yourself a priority is a priority.

## FACT #1: SUPERMEN AND SUPERWOMEN ARE **NOT** REAL

I know this may come as a shock; but in the real world, there is no such thing as superheroes. You simply cannot be all things to all people all the time, and you will make yourself insane trying. It is a senseless, hopeless cause. As someone astutely observed, "You can do anything—but not everything."[3]

Nevertheless, we have become programmed to think we can do it all, and we plunge headlong into life believing that we must. With ordinary human capacity, we try to accomplish the impossible. Herbert Prochnow summarized well our dilemma, "A person has to be a contortionist to get along these days. First of all he's got to keep his back to the wall and his ear to the ground. He's expected to put his shoulder to the wheel, his nose to the grindstone, keep a level head and both feet on the ground. And, at the same time, have his head in the clouds, so he can look for the silver lining."[4]

Today's world is much different from earlier generations. Perhaps you have found yourself calling or texting family members from various rooms of the same house. Or maybe you have found yourself saying, "What do you mean we don't communicate! Just yesterday, I faxed you a reply to the recorded message you left me on my answering machine!"[5]

We live in an impersonal, technology-crazed world and here are just a few of the signs:

- ☆ You've just tried to enter your password on the microwave.
- ☆ You have a list of fifteen phone numbers to reach your family of three.
- ☆ You call your son's beeper to let him know it's time to eat. . . .
- ☆ Your daughter sells Girl Scout cookies from her website.
- ☆ You chat several times a day with a stranger from South Africa, but haven't spoken with your neighbor next-door yet this year. . . .
- ☆ You pull up in your own driveway and use your cell phone to see if anyone is home. . . .
- ☆ You get an extra phone line so you can get phone calls.

✩ You start tilting your head sideways to smile.[6] :)

Unfortunately, in the craziness of our existence, we sometimes lose touch with the real meaning behind all that we do. We are so busy making money, playing taxi, coaching soccer, giving speeches, running errands, cleaning house, planning lessons, answering emails, and making phone calls that there is little time to enjoy the ones most precious to us. The Germans have a word for this kind of craziness: *Zerrissenheit*. It means "torn-to-pieces-hood," which is exactly what happens when we try to do too much.[7] We cannot long resist the centrifugal forces pulling at us from every side on the dizzying merry-go-round of life without suffering significant negative consequences.

The person who tries to do it all will, most likely, end up like my young son, who was trying to carry an armful of Popsicles upstairs. No sooner did he get his arms full than a few of the Popsicles fell to the floor. When he tried to pick them up, a couple more fell to the ground. Each time he got them all gathered up, one or two would slip from his grasp. After several attempts to collect them all, he exclaimed angrily, "Dumb popsicles!"

As an objective onlooker, it was obvious what the problem was and how to fix it—carry fewer popsicles. But to my overzealous son, the solution was not so simple. Determined to do more than he was capable, he failed to recognize or accept his personal contribution to the problem.

Similarly, when our own lives get too far out of whack, there is a tendency to blame those around us—"dumb" spouse, "dumb" children, "dumb" parents, "dumb" church, "dumb" employer. Perhaps we should look inward for the solution to many of our problems. Have we unwisely taken on more than we can handle? Do we need to delegate some of our tasks? Should we solicit help from others?

> A young boy was struggling unsuccessfully to move a heavy rock. His father stood nearby and finally asked why he wasn't using all his strength. The boy assured his dad that he was.
>
> "But why aren't you asking me to help?" said the father.
>
> Successful people use all their strength. That means they ask for help when they need it . . . and utilize all available resources to increase their power.
>
> The key to leadership is getting others around you involved—making them know their efforts are important to the common goal. The more you inspire them to do their part, the better things will turn out for all of you.[8]

Mothers, especially, must be cautious about doing too much. "For to be a woman is to have interests and duties raying out in all directions from the central mothercore, like spokes from the hub of a wheel."[9] How readily a mother's life becomes consumed with people and programs and projects. So much of what a mother does must be done. Therefore, she must carefully guard her time, being wary of taking on too many additional duties. Foolishly vying for the ever-elusive role of superwoman will only intensify zerrissenheit and leave you feeling incapable of doing anything well.

"We attempt sometimes to water a field, not a garden. We throw ourselves indiscriminately into committees and causes. Not knowing how to feed the spirit, we try to muffle its demands in distractions. Instead of stilling the center, the axis of the wheel, we add more centrifugal activities to our lives—which tend to throw us off balance."[10]

> In fact, there is . . . a new syndrome ascribed to working mothers called "Hurried Woman Syndrome". . . .
>
> This syndrome [i]s . . . due to the stress caused by trying to do too much, not being able to keep up with it, not feeling very accomplished at any of it, resenting anyone who has any expectations (like husband and children), and ending up feeling hostile and depressed. . . .
>
> Many married women with children are

wearing themselves down to the point that ill health and ill temper are the result. The problem is not with the demands of their husbands and children; the problem is with their notion of a full life. "Having it all" begins to approximate a "jack of all trades and a master of none." It is also a self-perpetuating trap. If the work is demanding and draining, and your time is limited and your temper isn't, guilt usually drives one toward more activity for children to "make up" for the neglect . . . . This translates into frenetic schedules of extra curricular activities, which end up overextending and stressing the children as well as the parents.[11]

This superhero mentality can really get us into a lot of trouble. Therefore, we must regularly evaluate our lives and carefully consider every new undertaking. A new job, a new location, or a new baby can put us on overload before we know it. We may need to eliminate or reduce some activities to compensate for the added stress these new endeavors create. For example, volunteering to teach Girl Scouts or serve on the PTA may not be such a good idea with a new baby on the way. Maybe you won't be able to coach soccer this year with the extra workload your promotion has created. Or perhaps you really don't have time to be on the city council, the school board, or the committee that plans your town's annual celebration with everything else that is going on in your life.

> Commitments are like flowers in a garden. If you over plant, none will thrive. . . .
>
> Some cures for the "too busy" blues: Serve on only one volunteer committee at a time; avoid taking calls during dinner; . . . do the things you're good at and delegate the things you're not good at; find your rhythm—for example, do you work better in the morning or later in the day?
>
> Devote your time to the things that matter most to you, and give yourself permission to get rid of the projects and even people that hinder you.[12]

On a daily basis there are choices to be made. If you spend all day working, running errands, gardening, or being busy with other projects, you will have to accept the fact that the house may not get cleaned as well as you would like—or maybe not at all; the lawn may not get mowed; some of the laundry may go undone; and dinner may be something simple that is thrown together at the last minute.

With three and a half acres, a variety of animals, and a large garden to care for, we spend a good part of the summer working outdoors. On busy outside days, the inside chores get a bit neglected, and mealtimes are not always a priority. Thank goodness for fresh garden produce that provides a quick fix to my summer meal-time predicaments.

At our house we also like to read books as a family. Some days when I sit down to read a chapter or two to the children, we get so caught up in the adventures of Billy and his two little red hounds in *Where the Red Fern Grows*; running through the woods with Jay Berry trying to catch that big monkey in *Summer of the Monkeys*; or flying around the world with James in a giant peach, that we read much longer than anticipated. Dinner on those nights gets a bit tricky—trying to throw something together at the last minute that doesn't look thrown together.

In contrast, some days I spend a good part of the day preparing my husband's favorite food or a special meal for a birthday child. On other days I spend most of my time typing at the computer—those days leave little time for stories, yard work, or fancy fixings.

Every day you need to ask yourself, "What are my priorities today?" Realizing that some things will be slighted or eliminated helps remove much of the guilt associated with not being able to do everything. Tomorrow you will have different priorities, and perhaps the things you neglect today will become priorities tomorrow. You cannot spend all day in the yard, at the kitchen stove, *and* on the computer. You simply cannot do it all.

Furthermore, do not feel as though you need to

become a composite of all the wonderful and worth-while things you see others doing. Concentrate on the talents and abilities that are uniquely yours without trying to do it all. "[You] want better for [your] children than a [parent] who exhausts herself with a perpetual race to the end of a never-ending to-do list."[13]

> Throw out any comparisons you make between what you and other [people] seem able to get done in their lives. You don't know what their behind-the-scenes situations might be like—their financial means, the things they don't get done, the support and help they have that you might not have, the price they pay elsewhere in their lives to get so much done. . . . Don't let a lengthy to-do list, however carefully and enthusiastically constructed be the primary dictator of the tone and pace of your days.[14]

In his book, *Don't Sweat the Small Stuff . . . and It's All Small Stuff,* Richard Carlson gives timely advice for reducing and eliminating. "Some things are worth sweating over. The tricky part is to determine what is really important and worthy of your energy and what constitutes the small stuff that causes needless worry and diminishes the quality of your life."[15]

Not long ago, I passed a young man while shopping. The message on his T-shirt caught my attention: "I can only be nice to one person a day. Today is not your day. Tomorrow is not looking too good either." That is the flippant teenage version of what I am trying to say—you cannot be all things to all people at all times.

Sometimes when my husband's eighty-year-old grandmother was feeling pressured by the projects in her life that were going undone, she would arbitrarily dismiss them by saying, "In the end, it won't matter anyway." And in the end, it didn't!

"There is no pleasure in having nothing to do. The fun is in having lots to do and not doing it."[16] It is perfectly acceptable to leave some things undone from time to time. Try it—it is very liberating and therapeutic. Someone once gave some excellent advice: "Do yourself a favor. Overlook at least two things today."[17] I know that can be a very difficult thing to do, especially when we have been conditioned to think otherwise.

Someone else has wisely counseled, "The main thing is to keep the main thing the main thing."[18] When you feel inclined to do more, ask yourself:

☆ What are the **B**enefits to myself or my family?
☆ Is it **E**ssential?
☆ Is it **S**ensible?
☆ How much **T**ime will it involve?

All things considered, is it the **BEST** thing

for everyone involved? Even some things that are worthwhile and meaningful may not be in your best interest. They may not be worth the sacrifice of time and energy that will be required of you and other family members. Furthermore, they may not be worth the added stress and turmoil they bring into your home.

This simple evaluation will help you more easily narrow down the activities and events in which you or other family members will be involved. Funneling out less important or unnecessary activities allows more time to focus on the things and people that really matter. In short, the main thing will become the main thing.

> Just because something is *good* is not a sufficient reason for doing it. The number of good things we can do far exceeds the time available to accomplish them. Some things are better than good, and these are the things that should command priority attention in our lives . . . .
>
> In choosing how we spend time as a family, we should be careful not to exhaust our available time on things that are merely good and leave little time for that which is better or best.[19]

Sometimes we get so caught up in the side streets of life that we lose focus of the main purpose of our journey. Becoming too distracted by unnecessary or unimportant detours will only result in roadblocks or dead ends to enduring happiness. Most of our lives are lived in the fast lane. Slow down. Recklessly speeding down the road of life or carelessly taking every exit—or event—you come upon is an accident waiting to happen. Excessively entering and exiting life's interstates creates unnecessary traffic jams and may prevent you from ever reaching your desired destination. The main thing is to carefully chart a course for your life that gets you where you really want to go. Then buckle up and enjoy the ride—without wishing for unnecessary excursions of every spectacle you encounter.

You can only do what you can do, and there will always be regrets about some things you did not or could not do. You simply cannot travel two separate paths simultaneously. The brevity and complexity of life forces decision and sacrifice.

Supermen and superwomen are fantasies. The half-mortal comic book characters can stay out all night rescuing children from burning buildings, jumping off enormous skyscrapers, and other fantastic feats of bravery . . . and still show up on time for their day jobs. It doesn't work that way for the rest of us. Being mortal means that we have limitations. If we are too intent on being the hero that saves the world, we will end up losing something of ourselves and our families. We cannot be all things to all people. It simply is not possible to save every starfish.

## FACT #2: NOT EVERYTHING WORTH DOING IS WORTH DOING WELL

I know this concept is inconsistent with everything you have been taught by parents, grandparents, teachers, or others of significance whose well-meaning advice you trusted. Most likely you heard various versions of their opposing opinions as a child: "If a job is worth doing, do it well or not at all;" "Do your best;" or "Give it your all." Perhaps you have even passed their words of wisdom on to your own children.

Doing a job well is definitely good advice for children who are still trying to develop healthy work ethics and build important character traits that will facilitate success in later years. Children need to push and stretch and challenge themselves. They need to learn to do things that are not pleasant or enjoyable and to do them well.

But this book is not for children. It is for adults with very busy lives who are feeling overworked and overwhelmed. The previous section discussed eliminating unnecessary activities from your life; but even after eliminating and reducing, you may still have more than you can handle.

Contrary to what you may have been taught—and may still believe—it simply is not possible or practical in your very busy adult world to do your best on every project every time. That does not mean, however, that you should never do anything well—just be reasonable and realistic in your expectations. It has been said, "A man would do nothing if he waited until he could do it so well that no one could find fault."[20] And someone else has facetiously observed, "Last week I saw a man who had not made a mistake in 4,000 years. He was a mummy in the British Museum."[21]

We are imperfect people living in an imperfect world. Do not expect perfection of everything you attempt. The perfectionist may have his life meticulously ordered, numbered, labeled, alphabetized, and color coded, but at what cost? Believing that you can or should or must do your best ALL the time is the source of much unnecessary stress, guilt, worry, depression, and physical ailments. For your own personal well-being, you must be willing to accept "good enough."

Two young brothers, yearning for adventure, decided to dig a hole through to the other side of the earth. With a couple of shovels, they went to work on a small patch of grass alongside their house.

A couple of older boys walked past and noticed the youngsters knee-deep in dirt. "Hey, what are you guys doing?" asked one boy.

"We're digging down to the other side of the earth," answered one of the brothers.

The older boys laughed at their folly. But the boys refused to give up.

They found a couple of dimes, a 1930s bottle, an old metal spring, and some unusual insects. But as night began to fall, it became clear that they were falling short of their goal.

Unbeaten, one boy remarked, "Well, maybe we can't dig through to the other side of the earth, but we sure found a lot of neat stuff!"

The youngsters had learned a simple but valuable lesson: If your goals are unrealistic, you may fail. But that shouldn't stop you from trying, for the road of unfulfilled dreams is often paved with treasures.[22]

Setting unrealistic goals creates feelings of anxiety and unrest. Be willing to settle for less. Life's richest rewards are not usually found in great big heaps at the end of brightly-colored rainbows. Rather, they are collected bit by bit along the path when we take time to enjoy the small and simple things of life.

Replace the notion of doing everything well with a new motto: "A second rate Something is better than a first rate Nothing."[23] You will be amazed at how quickly the stress diminishes. "I don't look to jump over seven-foot bars," Warren Buffet commented. "I look around for one-foot bars that I can step over."[24]

You don't have to do your very best all the time. You don't have to do the job better than it has ever been done before. You don't have to save every starfish. And you certainly don't need to live in the fast lane!

In other words, you don't have to get straight A's, have a picture-perfect house and yard, serve mouth-watering cuisine on a daily basis, raise perfectly well-behaved children, and have the most impressive Christmas display in the neighborhood. And, yes, it also means that it is perfectly fine to serve leftovers on paper plates to your guests, wear the same outfit two days in a row, water the flowers in your front yard dressed in bunny slippers, and take your children shopping in their Halloween costumes—even in July!

Sometimes we are so paralyzed by fear of failure, not measuring up, or not meeting perceived expectations that we fail to do anything. Fear is a hindrance to progress and success. It can have a crippling effect on our lives. Maybe we should care a little less about what other people think. When we aren't trying to impress anyone, we can be content with making an honest effort and performing an adequate job.

There are at least three lessons to be learned from the famous children's tale about the slow but steady turtle that beat the speedy hare.

First, so many people speed through life so quickly that they never enjoy the ride.

Next, Life really doesn't have a finish line where the first one there wins a prize.

Lastly, you can get the job done without unnecessary stress by taking the slower, scenic route.[25]

My personal motto for life is: "Not everything worth doing is worth doing well." I adapted this concept from a talk I heard years ago, and I regularly remind myself of this when I am going overboard on a project or when I am feeling guilty for not doing more.

You don't need to clean the oven, the bathtub, and behind the refrigerator just because you are having company for dinner. Likewise, the garden party will still be a success even if the lawn doesn't get edged—or mowed—and there are a few weeds in your flower beds. Furthermore, you do not need to outdecorate, outbake, and outdo all the neighbors at Christmas time. And there is no written law stating that all of your Christmas gifts need to be handmade—including matching pajamas for everyone in the family.

I actually made matching pajamas for my eight children one Christmas. I have to admit, there was a certain satisfying thrill at seeing my children all dressed alike on Christmas Day in outfits we had made ourselves, but my timing was not the best. We began this ambitious undertaking during the summer when my older children could help and simultaneously improve their sewing skills. In that regard, it was a worthwhile project. However, I was expecting baby number eight the end of September, and we were building a new home and preparing to move the first of November. It was an insanely hectic time, and my sewing project only added to the craziness. I should have known better.

Unnecessary stress and guilt take the fun out of life, and life was meant to be enjoyed. A wise person has noted, "Some people miss the message because they are too busy checking the spelling."[26] And someone else reminds us, "Life does not have to be regarded as a game in which scores are kept and somebody wins. If you are too intent on winning, you will never enjoy playing."[27]

## FACT #3: MAKING YOURSELF A PRIORITY IS A PRIORITY

Taking time for personal renewal and rejuvenation is absolutely crucial! In order to maintain some degree of sanity and well-being, you must make yourself a priority. After all, if you don't take care of yourself, who will?

> Traditionally we are taught, and instinctively we long, to give. . . . Eternally, [we spill ourselves] away in driblets to the thirsty, seldom being allowed the time, the quiet, the peace, to let the pitcher fill up to the brim. . . .
>
> We are hungry, and not knowing what we are hungry for, we fill up the void with endless

distractions, always at hand—unnecessary errands, compulsive duties, social niceties. . . . Suddenly the spring is dry; the well is empty. . . .

. . . If one sets aside time for a business appointment, a trip to the hairdresser, a social engagement, or a shopping expedition, that time is accepted as inviolable. But if one says: I cannot come because that is my hour to be alone, one is considered rude, egotistical or strange. . . .

Actually these are among the most important times in one's life. . . . Certain springs are tapped only when we are alone. . . .

When we start at the center of ourselves, we discover something worthwhile extending toward the periphery of the circle. We find again some of the joy in the now, some of the peace in the here.[28]

Obviously, this notion of focusing on self can be taken to the extreme. A life consumed with only selfish interests will never be a happy one. Service and sacrifice are essential elements of a fulfilled and joyful life. Interestingly, Mandarin Chinese has two separate and distinct words for selfish. "One means to do something that is beneficial to yourself and the other means to do something that is greedy, hoarding, or cruel."[29] Doing something nice for yourself is not greedy, hoarding, or cruel, rather it produces enormous benefits for yourself as well as those around you.

But too often we try so hard to be the perfect grandfather, grandmother, husband, wife, father, mother, son, daughter, brother, sister, neighbor, friend, employee, soccer coach, and PTA president that we leave no time for ourselves. You cannot give from an empty cup. When you give until there's nothing left to give, you will find yourself feeling angry, hurt, bitter, resentful, and depressed. Don't be afraid to turn off or ignore the TV, the computer, the telephone, and the doorbell to carve out a little quiet time for yourself.

It's "nice to be nice," but there's a problem. People-pleasers often take care of others at the expense of themselves and go to great lengths to avoid conflict. Activities that promote good health, like the daily walk, healthy food, and a good night's sleep are sacrificed when someone else is in need.

When your value is defined by what other people think about you, there will be times when you don't measure up. . . .

People pleasing is a learned behavior that you can unlearn. "No" is a complete sentence.

Take care of yourself. Do something that recharges your batteries every day, no matter what.

A healthy life is a life in balance. Treat yourself as nicely as you treat others.[30]

Years ago, I watched with interest as the men across the street poured cement for a new driveway. They worked intently for some time, and at last the job was finished. Then, in seeming celebration of their achievement, they stretched out on the lawn and spent the next three hours talking and laughing. Three hours! *What a waste of time!* I thought to myself. *Surely there are more productive ways to spend the day.*

However, as I went about my work that afternoon, I kept noticing the men whenever I passed my kitchen window. My day was typical of most days—cleaning up, changing diapers, fixing meals, wiping tears, refereeing arguments, more cleaning up, more diapers, more tears, and more arguments. I moved anxiously from one task to another, trying to cram as much as possible into the day. As the afternoon wore on, my initial indictment of the men across the street gradually turned to envy. In fact, I became almost resentful of their leisure time. For too long I had considered taking time for myself a luxury I could not afford. Suddenly I realized how wrong I was and how desperately I needed that precious personal time, and I resolved to do better.

On a daily basis we need to refill our personal reservoirs through prayer, study, meditation, goal setting, *and* by doing something personally rewarding—exercising, leisure reading, pursuing a hobby, taking a walk, or watching a sunset. "Breathe deeply, drink water, sleep peacefully, eat nutritionally, enjoy activity, give and receive love, be forgiving, practice gratitude, develop acceptance, nurture your spiritual side."[31] The following list for happiness offers suggestions for taking care of yourself. While it is certainly not all inclusive, it is an excellent starting point. Feel free to come up with your own ideas:

1. Keep only cheerful friends. The grouches pull you down.
2. Keep learning. Learn more about the computer, crafts, gardening, whatever. Never let the brain idle.
3. Enjoy the simple things.
4. Laugh often, long, and loud. Laugh until you gasp for breath.
5. Tears happen. Endure, grieve, and move on. The only person who is with you your entire life is you. Be ALIVE while you are alive.
6. Surround yourself with what you love, whether it's family, pets, keepsakes, music, plants, hobbies, whatever. Your home is your refuge.
7. Cherish your health. If it is good, preserve it. If it is unstable, work to improve it. If it is beyond what you can improve, get help.
8. Don't take guilt trips. Take a trip to the

mall, to the next county, to a foreign country, but NOT to where the guilt is.

9. Tell the people you love that you love them—at every opportunity.

10. And remember, there's no way you can look as bad as that person on your driver's license![32]

I knew a woman whose personal emotional outlet was a one-hour bubble bath while her husband watched their young children. During this time of renewal, she gave herself a manicure and a pedicure. She left the bathroom rejuvenated and refreshed and ready to take on her responsibilities once again.

Another woman I knew took one hour for lunch and a nap every day. And still another woman takes an entire day for herself every now and then. A man I know jogs and works out to relieve stress. Some people read, some build things, some fix things, some crochet, some take walks, and some weed flower beds or work in their gardens. Find what works for you.

For many years the only personal time I had was a few minutes of exercising every morning and a short nap every afternoon. With a regular cycle of pregnancies and newborns, that daily nap was crucial to my physical, emotional, and mental well-being. Thankfully, my husband and children recognized and respected this need. It was the only thing that got me through those difficult years.

Take time regularly—daily, if possible—to do whatever it is that you find rewarding and relaxing— without feeling guilty, making excuses, or apologizing. Get away from it all through dates, time out with friends, or other calming activities. It is especially important for mothers with young children to regularly get out of the house and away from the children. Long ago my husband recognized this need, and there have been very few Friday nights that we have not spent together away from home—even with newborns. Of necessity, the baby accompanied us the first several months; but at least we got away from the rest of the commotion at home.

"When one is a stranger to oneself then one is estranged from others too. If one is out of touch with oneself, then one cannot touch others."[33] Stay in touch with yourself through "[q]uiet time alone, contemplation, prayer, music, a centering line of thought or reading, of study or work. It can be physical or intellectual or artistic. . . . Arranging a bowl of flowers in the morning can give a sense of quiet in a crowded day."[34] Ironically, you will find that as you make time to fill your personal reservoir, there will be so much more of you to give to others.

Now, I know what you are probably thinking: *I don't have time for all the things I am supposed to be doing let alone taking time for naps, dates, bubble baths, and flower arranging!* The key to making time for yourself is scheduling and prioritizing. "You will never 'find' time for anything. If you want time you must make it."[35] You need to plan time for yourself the same way you plan for dentist appointments, soccer games, and business meetings. When *you* become a priority to *you*, good things will begin to happen.

For many years I had a desire to write. However, with my days full of diapers, dishes, and dirty laundry, there was no time for writing—or so I thought. Relentlessly, time marched on. One day it dawned on me that if I didn't make time for writing, it would never happen.

Shortly after the birth of my seventh child, my husband and I had a long conversation. I explained my desire to write and the impossible nature of doing that during the day with a house full of children. With all the hubbub going on around me, I couldn't even think a complete thought, let alone write a coherent sentence! At last, we came up with a plan. One night a week, immediately following dinner, I would lock my self away while my husband coordinated kitchen cleanup and bedtime.

When I say "lock," I mean it literally. An "open door" policy would have only subjected me to the constant demands and distractions of the children. Even with my husband's help, there were still children fussing and fighting just outside the door, children knocking on the door, and children calling "mommy, mommy" while poking their little fingers underneath the door. When my motherly sympathies got the best of me (or when the banging and the clanging and the crying became too distracting), I would open the door to see what terrible fate had befallen them. Before too long, my husband would discover that a child (or two) was missing; and he would quickly snatch them away, locking the door on the way out.

Those precious two or three hours a week for writing were not much, especially when the first several minutes of each week were spent refocusing my thoughts and coming up to speed on where I had left off the previous week. Then there were the occasional distractions—the banging, clanging, and crying. And from time to time, those weekly writing sessions were pre-empted by other activities—Cub Scout Pack Night, piano recitals, or other obligations. But, bit by bit, week by week, year after year, something eventually came from them.

Three years after my first "closed-door" writing session, I finished my first book. Three years later, I finished my second one. This is now my third book.

Time moves forward regardless of how we choose to fill it. You can spend a lifetime wishing for more money, more time, more opportunities, or more success, but nothing of substance comes from wishing. If you want things to happen, you must make them happen—a few minutes here, a few minutes there, an hour here, an hour there. You will be amazed at what can come from the combined efforts of those little spurts of time.

In order to have time for yourself, you must be willing to accept the fact that you will not be able to save every starfish you happen upon. And some things, of necessity, will only be done "good enough." Many of these things will be the important and necessary things of life. Some of them may even be meetings, events, and projects where you will be under the scrutiny of other people, sometimes a great many people. However, you will recognize that not every assignment deserves your very best effort. After all, not everything worth doing is worth doing well.

The following chapter will focus on various aspects of life, offering suggestions for cutting back, simplifying, and learning to accept "good enough."

## NOTES

1. Inspired by the work of Loren Eiseley; see *The Star Thrower* (New York: Random House, 1978), 171–73.

2. Unknown, Richard L. Evans, *Richard Evans' Quote Book,* (Salt Lake City: Publishers Press, 1980), 62.

3. David Allen, quoted by Keith H. Hammonds, "You Can Do Anything—But Not Everything," fastcompany.com, http://

www.fastcompany.com/magazine/34/allen.html?page=0%2C2

4. Herbert Prochnow, *The Public Speaker's Treasure Chest* (New York: Harper & Brothers Publishers, 1942), 108.

5. Unknown, "This 'n' That," *Educators Mutual* 25, no. 8 (August 2005): 8.0

6. Unknown, "Stress Less," *Hope Health Letter* 23, no. 6 (June 2003): 3.

7. Anne Morrow Lindbergh, *Gifts From the Sea* (New York: Pantheon Books, 1955), 50.

8. Adapted from *Puppies for Sale, and Other Inspirational Tales* by Dan Clark, in "The Key to Strength," *Educators Mutual* 25, no. 6 (June 2005): 5

9. Anne Morrow Lindbergh, *Gifts From the Sea,* 22.

10. Ibid., 46.

11. Dr. Laura Schlessinger, *The Proper Care & Feeding of Husbands* (New York: HarperCollins, 2006), 21, 23.

12. Edward M. Hallowell, *CrazyBusy: Overstretched, Overbooked, and About to Snap!* in "Stress Less," *Educators Mutual* 26 no. 11 (November 2006): 7.

13. Debra Sansing Woods, *It's Okay to Take a Nap* (Springville, UT: Cedar Fort, Inc., 2008), 11.

14. Ibid., 10.

15. Michael Olpin and Margie Hesson, *Stress Management for Life: A Research-Based, Experiential Approach* (Belmont, CA: Thomson Brooks/Cole, 2007), 20

16. Mary Wilson Little, "Body, Mind, and Soul," *Hope Health Letter,* 24, no. 10 (October 2004): 8.

17. M. J. Ryan, "Body, Mind, and Soul," *Hope Health Letter* 24, no. 2 (February 2004): 8.

18. Stephen R. Covey, quoteworld.com, http://www.quoteworld.org/quotes/3234 (accessed August 29, 2008).

19. Dallin H. Oaks, "Good, Better, Best," *Ensign,* Nov. 2007, 104, 105.

20. John Henry Cardinal Newman, "This 'n' That," *Hope Health Letter* (2004).

21. H. L. Wayland, "Body, Mind, and Soul," *Educators Mutual* 25, no. 4 (April 2005): 8.

22. Adapted from *Riches of the Heart,* by Steve Goodier, in "It's the Journey that Counts," *Hope Health Letter* 24, no. 6 (June 2004): 5.

23. Unknown, *Richard Evans' Quote Book,* 62.

24. Unknown, "This 'n' That," *Educators Mutual* 25, no. 6 (June 2005): 8.

25. Z. Altug, *The Anti-Aging Fitness Prescription,* quoted in "The Tortoise and the Hare," *Educators Mutual* 26, no. 9 (September 2006): 6.

26. Unknown, "Body, Mind, and Soul," *Hope Health Letter* 23, no. 11 (Nov. 2003): 8.

27. Thomas Merton, "This 'n' That," *Hope Health Letter* 24, no. 3 (March 2004): 8.

28. Anne Morrow Lindbergh, *Gift from the Sea,* 39, 41, 42, 44, 122.

29. Debra Sansing Woods, *It's Okay to Take a Nap,* 96.

30. Vicki Rackner, "Doc Talk," *Educators Mutual* 25, no. 6 (June 2005): 4.

31. *Educators Mutual* 25, no. 6 (June 2005): 8.

32. Unknown, "How to Stay Young," *Educators Mutual* 24, no. 12 (December 2004): 5.

33. Anne Morrow Lindbergh, *Gift from the Sea,* 38.

34. Ibid., 50.

35. Charles Buxton, *Richard L. Evans' Quote Book,* 100.

# Sometimes "Good Enough"
# Is Good Enough

## ⭐ MEALS

A friend related a story about the time she went out of town overnight, leaving her husband to care for their children in her absence. Since her husband was not known for his culinary abilities, my friend naturally assumed that he would opt for an easy dinner by purchasing pizza or hamburgers.

Upon returning, she asked the children, "So, what did Dad fix for dinner?"

Unruffled, the children replied, "Nothing. He just opened a bag of chips, and we all stood around and ate it." And they all survived! (I hope they were nacho cheese chips—then they would at least get two of the four food groups.)

As a young girl taking home economics in junior high school, I learned about the four food groups. Then and there I set what I considered a worthwhile goal: the meals I prepared for my future family would not only be aesthetically appealing, but they would always include food from all four groups. Then I had children. In the craziness of trying to catch every starfish—running here and rushing there on planned and unplanned errands, chaotic schedules, demanding newborns, and a houseful of children, my naïve, juvenile goal has not always matched reality.

Several years ago, a friend taught me a completely new definition of the four food groups. She classified them as: boxed, bottled, canned, and frozen. I remember her advice whenever I am stressing over a meal that is a bit less than complete.

While standing at the kitchen stove frying homemade onion rings recently, my young son entered the room and wondered aloud, "Is that all we're having for dinner?" (Had my meals really deteriorated to that level?) Teasingly, I told him that it was but quickly assured him that we would still be getting all the necessary nutrients from the meal. I then sarcastically began to enumerate the many nutritious qualities of an onion ring.

First, the onion itself is a vegetable. That was a definite benefit. Second, the batter I dipped them in was made of cornmeal—another vegetable (or would that be a grain?). It also contained milk, eggs, and flour, which covered the remaining food groups—dairy, meat, and grains. (The flour I was using was even whole wheat, which improved its value dramatically.) To complete the food pyramid, I was frying the onion rings in oil, which more than satisfied the daily intake requirements for oil and sugars. And finally, we would be dipping the onion rings in fry sauce, which was made from ketchup, which was made from tomatoes, another vegetable—or fruit, depending on how you look at it. Three vegetables in one food! I had never realized that onion rings were such a complete meal— we should have them more often.

As I passed a man in the grocery aisle years ago, he said to me while waving a package of ramen noodles, "This is the cheapest meal you can find." I think he was right. Not only is it inexpensive and easy, but I have figured out that if you add a few frozen vegetables, you almost have a complete meal!

Sometimes, especially in those early years, I made mealtime too complicated. While you cannot argue the absolute necessity of food, it did not take me long to learn that not every meal can—or should be—gourmet delight. In fact, many of my meals are far from gourmet. Saturday lunch at our house is whatever you can find or served buffet style by emptying out the contents of the refrigerator.

Over the years I have learned a few tricks about mealtime. First, a tablecloth turns an ordinary meal into something special. (But we don't use one every day—think of the laundry!) And candlelight enhances a meal even more. Somehow everything tastes better in the flickering glow of candlelight, and your children will remember the magic of the moment long after the menu has been forgotten.

Second, take turns or work together when preparing meals. This will dramatically diminish the amount of time spent in the kitchen. Not only are important life skills learned while grating, grinding, chopping, and dicing, but much of family love and unity can be developed while washing broccoli with your four-year-old or buttering French bread with your ten-year-old. More than a meal is made in those few precious moments teaching a child to cook.

And, third, whenever I prepare soup, spaghetti, or a casserole, I make enough for at least two meals. It really doesn't take much longer to double or triple a recipe, and it is wonderful to have those "planned-overs" for another day. Unfortunately, I think my family sometimes feels like the man reminiscing about his own childhood: "The most remarkable thing about my mother is that for 30 years she served the family nothing but leftovers. The original meal has never been found."[1] Still, there is nothing better than leftovers—especially if you are the one preparing dinner; and I will continue to serve them as long as I do the cooking. If anyone complains, I would be more than happy to let them cook the next meal.

Learn to simplify. Years ago, when all the children

accompanied me to the grocery store, we usually went first thing in the morning, arriving home at lunchtime. Naturally, the children were tired and hungry, but I was too busy putting away groceries to prepare a meal. So, we ate lunch right out of the grocery sacks— a banana, a cracker, some cheese. We called it "a funny lunch," and it was "good enough" for my children. In fact, they loved it! I never bothered to tell them I was too tired and too stressed to do more.

And some nights I just consider myself lucky if I have something on the table when my husband gets home in the evening. The larger my family has become, the less time I have had to focus on fancy meals and new recipes. Increasingly, I have found myself falling back on the tried and tested recipes that are fast and easy and that I know my family likes. I have become quite expert at preparing meals that seem to take considerable effort but that can be thrown together in a rush shortly before my husband walks through the door. (Then he never knows we spent the day reading stories—unless the children tell.)

As a matter of fact, I was sitting in the living room reviewing a final draft of this book when I noticed my husband pull in the driveway. "I better get something for dinner!" I exclaimed in alarm. And what a dinner it was! My oldest son, who knew the content of this book, made it quite clear that sometimes a little more focus on the meal might be a good idea. He was even brazen enough to suggest that sometimes "good enough" was *not* good enough!

Despite the downsizing of our delectable dining dishes, I still do get those creative, culinary urges from time to time that send me to the kitchen for hours—mixing and measuring while making pies, bread, or cinnamon rolls from scratch. While I can get really excited about turning a meal into a masterpiece, I also know that it is perfectly fine to serve toasted cheese sandwiches and tomato soup or macaroni and cheese and hotdogs to my family occasionally. Some nights that will just have to be "good enough." And, as much as I hate to admit it, sometimes we don't even have a vegetable!

Over the years, I have learned that *what* you have for dinner is not nearly as important as *who* you have for dinner. There is great power and strength that comes from eating together as a family. In fact, the National Center on Addiction and Substance Abuse has found that children who eat dinner with their families are less likely to smoke, drink, use drugs, be depressed, develop eating disorders, or consider suicide. And teens who eat dinner with their families are more likely to get A's and B's in school.

There is something about a shared meal that anchors a family even on nights when the food is fast and the talk is cheap and everyone has someplace else they'd rather be . . . . On those evenings when the mood is right and the family lingers . . . you get a glimpse of the power of this habit and why [it] . . . acts as a kind of vaccine, protecting kids from all manner of harm.[2]

The simplest meal—a bag of chips—eaten at the kitchen counter in the company of loved ones is more satisfying than the richest, most extravagant cuisine consumed in silence and solitude. "What your children really want for dinner is you."[3]

## ✪ CLEANING HOUSE

Albert Einstein once remarked, "If a cluttered desk is a sign of a cluttered mind, of what then, is an empty desk?"[4]

While I do not completely agree with his premise, it is worth considering. In moderation, a certain amount of clutter is a sign of productivity and progress. You cannot cook, sew, or build things without creating clutter. I hate to think of a home where no one ever worked on projects or got creative in the kitchen.

Little children also love to be busy, which often results in an assortment of objects lying around as they go about their daily "work." Through building, creating, and playing, children imitate the world around them. The "messes" they make are actually miniature models of real life and a child's attempt to understand it. I know it isn't easy to focus on the education that is occurring when the room looks like a cyclone just went through and you are stepping and stumbling over and around the debris left in its wake. However, keep in mind that the scattered remains really are tangible evidence of your child's learning and growth.

Children need to be children. And somehow, being children means rooms will be strewn about in chaotic fashion with Lincoln Logs and Legos, and Barbies, buggies, and baby dolls. It means dirty footprints across your newly-installed carpet; crayon and pencil drawings on your freshly-painted walls; and dirty fingerprints on your just-cleaned windows and mirrors. With young children, it simply is not practical to expect the house to be clean all the time.

And yet, having a clean house is one of my favorite things in all the world. But even this worthy goal can be taken to the extreme. With each additional child, my goal of tidiness has become increasingly more difficult to maintain. Often it is more of a personal wish than anything else. You would not believe the amount of odds and ends ten children bring into a house. Trying to keep up with it is harder than saving starfish!

One particularly busy day of cleaning up after children, I had an epiphany of sorts: *As long as you have children there will always be something out of place. If you let it, cleaning up after your children will turn into a full-time job, and you will always be picking up and putting away.* Then I wondered to myself, *Is that the way I want to spend their childhood?*

When my children were younger and I realized that I was putting the same toys away every night and they were getting the same toys out every morning, it got to be a bit tedious. Some nights when I was too tired and too stressed to deal with it, I just pushed the toys into a pile in the corner of the room. At least then the room felt clean when I got up in the morning— and that was "good enough." I also got in the habit of picking up a few things to put away when I went down the hall, into the garage, or to the basement. It cuts down on the clutter, and I don't have a huge mess to deal with at one time.

With a great deal of effort, I have learned not to stress too much over the fact that the room I just cleaned is already being destroyed. I plan specific cleanup times throughout the day—breakfast, lunch, dinner, and bedtime—and I don't fret about disorder in the meantime. It has been hard, but I have learned to walk around it, over it, or away from it in order to move on to more important things. I have come to the conclusion that I could spend my children's growing-up years cleaning up, but what would I have to show for it? The house would still be messy again tomorrow.

A compulsive cleaner is never content because

there will always be something dirty or out of place. "In housekeeping, more is not always better. Order and cleanliness should not cost more than the value they bring in health, efficiency, and convenience."[5]

> We live in a culture focused on neatness and organization, but being a little messy may actually be good for you. Super neat people must constantly work at staying in control. Being a little messy, however, allows more flexibility and may make it easier to deal with unexpected events. 'If you're stressed it may be because you're spending three hours a day trying to be neat and organized. . . . Cut that time in half and enjoy the time you free up doing something you've always wanted to do.' "[6]

At our home, Saturday is cleaning day. Each child has specific housecleaning chores with specific expectations about how those chores will be completed. As soon as breakfast is over, everyone scatters in different directions to complete their assigned tasks, and for a few hours every Saturday, we enjoy a wonderfully clean house.

Furthermore, each morning my children are expected to make their beds, put away their clothes, and tidy their rooms. We also do daily touch ups and maintenance throughout the house. But with a large family, I have learned not to look too closely at the kitchen floor or the bathroom sinks during the week!

When you clean, make the most of your cleaning time. Work efficiently—dovetailing, multi-tasking, and planning the most effective use of your day. On a daily basis, a quick tidying up is usually sufficient. Then move on to other things.

Learn to take shortcuts. The extra refrigerator in my garage had needed a cleaning for some time and was really starting to bother me. On impulse one day, I decided to squeeze in a quick cleaning when I had a little time. I knew at the outset that there was not time to give it the really thorough cleaning that it normally receives—walking back and forth from the garage to the kitchen sink carrying drawers and shelves to wash in warm, soapy water.

Instead, I took the drawers to the kitchen, leaving the shelves and food in the refrigerator. Shuffling the food around on the shelves—cleaning half the shelf, then moving everything to the other side and cleaning the other half—I managed to do a pretty good cleaning job in a fraction of the time it normally took. *Wow!* I thought to myself. *It really doesn't need to take half the afternoon to clean the fridge.*

Even though this clever technique would never make it to any professional cleaning books, it was "good enough" for me. In the final analysis, it really doesn't matter what the professionals think because they will never see the inside of my refrigerator anyway. I am the only one who will ever know how it was cleaned. What really matters is that it was clean enough to fool my husband and children. And that is not hard to do because they aren't looking for dirt when they open the refrigerator!

The one thing I have finally come to accept is that clutter is part of raising a family. Someone is always taking something out of its tidy little spot and carelessly shoving it back in random order. Often I open a drawer or a closet—the one I just cleaned last week—to find it is already a mess. Things are jamming up in the drawer and falling out at me from the closet. What I really want to do is lash out with something like, "Why can't people put things back the way they found them?" or "Why can't we ever have anything nice around here?" That response gets no satisfactory answers and solves no long-term problems. So, instead, I close my eyes, clench my teeth, and say miserably to myself, *It won't **always** be like this.* Then I close the drawer or the closet and go on with life. I learned long ago that if I stood around fuming about everything that was out of place, I would never get anything done. Besides, the most important part of having children is enjoying them. That means putting up with a little dirt and dust now and then.

I once had a friend say, "My house is clean enough to be healthy, but dirty enough to be happy." I think that is a good balance, especially with young children.

Another mother once commented, "If you come to see me, come anytime; if you come to see my house, make an appointment." We all have clutter from time to time, so what is the big deal? You don't need to turn three shades of red and apologize profusely if someone stops by and catches your house with that "lived-in" look. After all, that is what we do there.

Still, I must confess, my secret wish is that someday there will be a place for everything and everything will be tucked neatly away in its place. And at times I find myself fantasizing: *When all the children are gone, I will wash down all the walls, patch all the scrapes and scratches, clean out all the drawers and cupboards, and everything will be just the way I want it.* When that day actually comes, however, I wonder if I might not want to leave a few of the nicks and notches as tender reminders of days gone by. Ironically, along with those irksome irregularities will be fond memories that I will probably come to cherish as the years roll on.

A child-friendly house is a happy house. Immaculate is for museums and places where there are no children. For now, I will be content with "good enough"—carefully stepping over . . . and around . . . and away.

## ☆ HOLIDAYS AND SPECIAL OCCASIONS

What has happened to the Norman Rockwell Christmases of yesteryear? They were picture-perfect—no stress, no worry, no endless errands, or crazy last-minute shopping. It was a simpler time. It was a happier time.

Families spent the holidays stringing popcorn for the tree, baking goodies, and singing carols. There were no expectations of a room full of toys and expensive gadgets and gizmos. Children would be delighted to find an orange, some candy, or a small gift on Christmas morning. Dinner would be the highlight of the day—a goose, a ham, or a turkey and some bread pudding or homemade pumpkin pie. The focus of the season was friends and family.

While creating holiday traditions is definitely worth doing, we must be careful about overdoing it. Learn to enjoy the simple things. Don't get so caught up in the hustle and bustle of trying to catch every starfish that you fail to notice the salty smell of the sea, the sunrise on the horizon, the gentle lapping of the ocean on the seashore, or the feel of the sand between your toes. In other words, don't get so caught up in your Christmas to-do list that you fail to notice all the wonderful sights and sounds and smells of this magical season.

For many of us, December has become one of the most dreaded months of the year. I was talking to a mother one day about Christmas and she said, "I just can't wait until it's over. I know I shouldn't say that, but that's how I feel." I knew exactly how she felt even though Christmas at our house is not extravagant.

When I was first married, my complete collection of homemade or hand-me-down Christmas decorations fit in one box. Today I have an entire closet stuffed with decorations. It takes two days just to set everything out. Interestingly, however, I don't enjoy Christmas any more with a houseful of decorations than I did with one small box. In fact, in some ways, I enjoy it less.

Furthermore, the first several years of our marriage my husband was in graduate school and the older children grew up not expecting a lot for Christmas. We have tried to be reasonable with our purchases in subsequent years. Still, shopping for ten children, a husband, my husband's co-workers, parents, extended family, neighbors, and friends can make the season rather hectic.

During the Christmas rush, I often find myself wondering, *Why is this most wonderful time of year the most dreaded and does it have to be this way?* The reason is obvious; the solution is not.

Most of the month of December is filled with shopping, wrapping, exchanging . . . more shopping . . . more wrapping . . . more exchanging. We drive ourselves crazy trying to buy the latest item to impress our nearly unimpressionable children even more this year than the year before. Every year we buy bigger and better to satisfy their ever-growing appetites for the newest toy or gadget, creating a greedy, vicious cycle that has us spiraling out of control.

One couple I know discussed at length how they would do Christmas before having children. Both parents came from rather humble circumstances with very simple Christmases, and they decided to raise their children in a similar fashion. Each child would receive one Santa gift, one parent gift, and one book. On Christmas Eve each child got new pajamas to wear to bed on that special night. That was it. I marveled at how simple they had made it.

At our home on Christmas morning when the children are rummaging through their stockings and looking at the gifts Santa left unwrapped, I think to myself: *This should be enough. If there were no other presents, this would still be a nice Christmas. Why do they need more?*

There are no easy answers and no wide-spread solutions to this growing dilemma, but we can choose to diminish the delirium in our own families. We can choose to cut back on the commercialism of Christmas and focus more on activities that bring us closer as families. We can think less of Santa and more of Christ. We can teach our children to reach out to others in meaningful ways, thus helping them understand that it truly is more blessed to give than to receive.

One of our Christmas traditions is to deliver

goodies to the neighbors while singing, "We Wish You a Merry Christmas" on their doorstep. One year we decided to visit several widows in the neighborhood. Naturally, they invited us in, and we spent time visiting at each home. The gratitude of the women was contagious, and we found ourselves lingering longer than anticipated. Arriving home late that evening, I noticed something different about the children. There was less quarreling, less teasing, less complaining. There was a more subdued atmosphere about them, and my husband and I took the opportunity to have them reflect on how they were feeling and what had caused those feelings. Without hesitation, they acknowledged that they felt happy because they had done something nice for someone else. It occurred to me then that this feeling of quiet peace was what Christmas was all about, and I determined that night that we would strive to have more of that in our home during the Christmas season.

As a result, the next year I cut back on the gifts for my children and finished the shopping and wrapping early in the month, leaving plenty of time for spreading Christmas cheer. We spent several evenings caroling to neighbors and widows. At each widow's home, we enjoyed an extended visit that included a short Christmas message, solos or duets on the piano—if they owned one, and a hug from each of us. I knew this activity had been successful when I overheard my five-year-old say to her older brother, "I like visiting the widows. I wish we could go every night."

Without the pressure of last-minute shopping, we also had more time for other activities—reading Christmas stories, pulling taffy, and making sugar cookies. It had been years since we had made sugar cookies at Christmas; it was just too stressful. But this year, we spent a wonderful afternoon cutting, baking, and decorating a kitchen full of cookies. I let my children punch out the various shapes by themselves, not even stressing over the fact that they weren't making the best use of the cookie dough. And, surprisingly, all of the teddy bears ended up with two legs and two arms and all the stars had five points—without any adult supervision. Five-year-old Marissa's cookies had half-inch thick frosting and great globs of sprinkles, but even that didn't bother me. I was amazed at my own level of tolerance and patience over things that would have normally been stressful and irritating.

This experience helped me realize how upside down and backwards Christmas had become. I had been cutting back on the most meaningful aspects of Christmas to make room for that which was less important. Christmas is not about things. It is about people and memories and traditions.

Somehow, though, it is often the things that take priority. I never cease to be amazed at the time and energy we spend buying treasures for our children that they really don't need or appreciate, and which will, most likely, be lost or broken by the end of the week. And if it isn't lost or broken, you just have to find a place to store it.

Too many parents shower gifts on their children that they really can't afford, spending a good part of the next year paying for them. It makes no sense at all. We would never act with such disregard for common sense on any other day of the year. You will enjoy the day after Christmas much more if there is no sickening realization that you must now figure out a way to pay for that one wildly insane spending spree.

Even if you can afford to do more, do your children really need it? In an era of ever increasing self-gratification, should parents be encouraging selfishness? After all, the "reason for the season" is for looking out, not in. Teaching the principle of self-*less*-ness is the best and longest-lasting gift any parent can give—and that is more than "good enough."

**Then there's the Easter Bunny.** Do we lose a little of the Easter spirit by focusing too much on bunnies and baskets and not enough on rebirth and renewal? I marvel at the enormous Easter baskets filled with toys and treats. Do our children really need all of that? I believe it is an unnecessary expense for parents and an unnecessary indulgence of our children.

My children get a little bunny made from a Twinkie or a coconut snowball with a few jelly beans or other candy sprinkled on the table beside it. These are set out Friday night to be eaten on Saturday, thereby leaving Easter Day to focus on its most important meaning. When my children wonder why their friends get more, I make up some lame excuse such as, "I guess the Easter Bunny runs out of goodies by the time he gets to our house." So far that response has been "good enough," and we have managed to get through the season without any negative consequences.

**Halloween used to be a big deal at our house.** We began talking about it early in the month and had the costumes ready long before the special day. When my older children were young, I even planned matching costumes for them. One year the two boys were wizards and the two girls were witches. Another year, the boys were devils and the girls were angels. One time they were all bugs. We stuffed black garbage bags with newspaper and taped colored paper dots to the bags. (Yes, we had to cut out all the dots.)

The more children I had, the less elaborate the costumes became. Then one year it all came to a crashing halt. Our seventh baby was due soon and coming up with creative Halloween costumes was not the most pressing issue, at least for me. On the afternoon of Halloween—just hours before the donning of costumes—I told the children to pick something, anything, out of the dress-up box in the basement and put it on.

They spent the next couple of hours parading in and out of the kitchen modeling a variety of possibilities. At length, everyone came up with an outfit that was "good enough," and we were off. As I reflected on that evening, I realized how complicated I had been making this already hectic holiday by spending too much time planning and stressing and preparing for an event where "anything goes." It really didn't matter what they wore. Most of the time their costumes were covered by coats anyway. Besides, the children had just as much fun in their thrown-together outfits as the ones I spent hours creating. So, I quit going to all the fuss.

**What about birthdays?** Birthdays are particularly special for children. After all, it is the one day of the year to celebrate them. But if we laden our children with gifts as if they were the kings or queens of some country, it sends the wrong message. They grow up with unrealistic expectations about themselves and the world they live in. This distorted view of reality will only bring disappointment in later years when they discover that the world does not revolve around them or when their future financial situation does not allow for such extravagance.

A friend told the story of a young boy who, using his imagination, turned an ordinary magic marker into a jet plane. Eventually it evolved into a rocket ship. He spent hours launching the marker into space and zooming it around the house. Noticing his inclination towards planes and rockets, his parents decided he would have more fun with something more realistic. So, they bought several toy replicas. The lad amused himself with his new toys for a few days but eventually returned to playing with the marker. The "magic" in that marker came from the images created in his own mind and were not limited to one shape or size as were the other toys.

A stick of any size readily becomes a sword or a gun for little boys, and little girls manage to play baby with a variety of objects—their stuffed animals, the family cat, or the balding baby doll from the basement with only one arm. And, to the chagrin of many mothers, they sometimes prefer the tattered, shabby one over their fancy new one. Years ago, baby dolls were made of cornstalks from the family garden, and little girls spent many happy hours playing with them. Have you ever noticed that very young children derive as much—if not more—pleasure from the wrapping paper, the ribbons and bows, and the boxes that enclose their gifts as they do from the gifts themselves? It really doesn't take much to please a child.

For many years I went to great effort to make elaborately-decorated cakes for my children's birthdays. I spent hours mixing, baking, frosting, and designing fancy borders and flowers—snapping at my children if they peered too closely or pointed a finger that threatened to destroy my masterpiece. While I enjoyed the finished product, it was time consuming and stressful. As the number of children increased, along with the demands on my time, I found cake decorating less and less enjoyable. One year, when I was particularly busy, I decided to let my three boys with November birthdays decorate their own cakes. I must admit, it took some effort to convince myself I was not being a negligent mother.

However, my boys were thrilled with the idea and had a great time decorating with candy corn and gum drops. The enthusiastic way they tackled the project demonstrated clearly that I had not been negligent. In fact, they enjoyed it so much that I decided to let my other children decorate their cakes as well.

We have now started a new tradition in our home—one which has freed up some of my time and which is rewarding and enjoyable for the children. They make plans for their cakes weeks ahead of time. There is much eager anticipation before baking the cake and much laughing and chattering while cutting and frosting and decorating. The end result is usually not much to look at, but it is "good enough" for my children.

There was a time when I would have cringed to display such sloppily-made birthday cakes—complete with large crumbs of cake in the frosting and some of the bare cake showing through the frosting. What a disaster! Interestingly enough, the children don't seem to notice. To them it is the perfect culmination to their special day. I have come to realize that it is not the appearance of the cake that matters most but the process that went into making it. As much as I hate to admit it, I believe their very amateur cakes will be remembered best and cherished most.

Slow down and cut back. A few presents and a few little treats are "good enough" for those special occasions. Our children don't need as much as we think they do. I think they would be just as happy—if not more so—with less. If you want to give them more, give them more of yourself—a happier, less uptight self. That is what they need more than all the things money can buy.

## ⭐ LESSONS AND PRESENTATIONS

I once saw a movie where the mother was in the kitchen with a chain saw carving out an enormous ice sculpture to be used as a centerpiece for the lesson she would be giving the next day. Absurd in its depiction, this sarcastic portrayal is, unfortunately, not far from the reality we sometimes create for ourselves.

There is nothing like teaching a class or giving a presentation to get those creative juices flowing. Teaching a class is certainly worth doing, but does it always need to include a fancy tablecloth, extravagant centerpieces, color-coordinated handouts, and tasty treats? Let some of the starfish go by going without the extra frills, and focus instead on the message you will be giving. That will be "good enough."

Not long ago, I was responsible for planning a meeting. The agenda included a training session followed by refreshments. Each of the three presenters was to bring some kind of dessert, and I had planned weeks ahead of time what I would make.

However, on the morning of the meeting, I woke feeling a bit pressed for time. At 11:00 I needed to pick up my son for an orthodontic appointment, and afterwards there were several errands that had to be done that day. Then I remembered something I had forgotten to type for the meeting. I figured there would be time to type it when I returned that afternoon, but . . . that was when I had planned to do my baking. Now I was faced with a dilemma. Should I spend the afternoon typing or making treats?

I thought about the chocolate chip cookie dough my daughter had mixed up a couple days earlier which had not been baked. The dough was still in the refrigerator. There was the solution to my problem—enabling me get both the treats and the typing done that afternoon.

*But would that be good enough?* I wondered. *After all, how impressive were chocolate chip cookies?*

I vacillated back and forth for most of the morning—should I make the more impressive refreshments I had planned, or should I settle for chocolate chip cookies? At length I decided that under the circumstances chocolate chip cookies would have to be "good enough."

Thankfully, the other two women came through with wonderful goodies that made everyone *ooh* and *ahh*—and I was grateful. Nevertheless, as I thought about this incident on the way home, it occurred to me that the focus of the evening was not on the treats but on the training. However, in my eagerness to excel, I had nearly lost sight of that important fact. There would be other times when the focus of an event would be the food but not tonight. *What's more,* I concluded, *even if all of us had made chocolate chip cookies, it would have been "good enough."*

Several years ago I was responsible for planning a daddy-daughter activity. Initially, I came up with the idea of a hoe down—complete with a chuck wagon dinner, checkered tablecloths, matching plates and cups, and square dancing. For several months, I worked out the details in my mind. In fact, I almost bought the tablecloths when I saw them at the store one day.

Then, just weeks before the event, I came to an abrupt halt. *Wait a minute!* I told myself. *You have ten children, including a new baby, and you're trying to finish writing a book. You don't have time for this. You would knock yourself out for days trying to pull this together.* It took some doing, but I finally convinced myself that all of that effort was not in my best emotional interest.

Instead, I decided to have the girls play three-legged baseball with their dads. All that activity required was a bat, a ball, and some rope to tie their legs together. For snacks we had popcorn in cute little bags, peanuts, and root beer floats.

This activity took very little preparation and created only a fraction of the stress of the original plan. The girls and their dads had a great time, and I got many compliments on the event. No one knew that there had been another plan, and no one was disappointed.

It is great to magnify your calling, but have you ever noticed what happens when a magnifying glass is put under too much heat? It can actually start a fire. You too will experience burn out if the heat is always on.

Creative juice can be sweet and satisfying, but too much of it will leave a bitter taste in your mouth. Impressive is certainly impressive, and sometimes that is just the effect you want. But don't forget that impressing others requires an impressive amount of time, effort, and sometimes money. If you turn every activity into a major event, you will find yourself turning sour on life. In contrast, simple is simple. Sometimes that is "good enough."

## ⭐ ERRANDS AND APPOINTMENTS

We had just moved and were unfamiliar with the dentists and doctors in our new area. Someone recommended a dentist thirty minutes away; and, without even thinking, off we went. On the second or third trip, I wondered about several of the offices we passed along the way. Surely, there were other equally-competent dentists much closer to home. At length, the practical side of me took over, and I decided to try the new dentist who had recently set up practice just minutes from home. He turned out to be excellent. Not only have I have been pleased with his work, but I have been delighted with the time I have saved commuting back and forth halfway across the valley.

Unless you have a particularly compelling reason for visiting a particular professional, chances are the one just around the corner or down the street will be equally as good as the one clear across town. Spare yourself the additional commute and the headache of traffic by finding someone closer. Most likely, that will be "good enough."

Furthermore, when you are out and about, plan your day to run several errands at the same time, thus eliminating the need for multiple trips. (You can save more starfish by picking up several of them at once.)

Make a list of errands to be done and the best order in which to do them so you don't spend a lot of time backtracking. And before leaving home for an impromptu errand, ask yourself, "Is the errand I am about to run really necessary? Can I make do without it? Could it wait until tomorrow or the next time I will be out?"

When you do find yourself buzzing around town, you can use the time for pondering and planning or listening to books on CD. If a child accompanies you, turn off the radio and the videos and put away the headphones and cell phones. The disadvantage of electronic equipment is that someone sitting right beside you can be miles away mentally. Being alone with your youngster provides prime time to connect and discuss things important to him. It is amazing what you can learn about your children in the few minutes it takes to run an errand or drive someone to practice. With so much to do and so little time, don't overlook those precious one-on-one occasions with your child.

When traveling with the family, pass the time by singing songs, reading stories, or playing car games. We have discovered that keeping children distracted lessens the boredom that often leads to a variety of negative behaviors requiring disciplinary action. One of our favorite companions for long drives is a nice big book with plenty of action. Since reading aloud requires silence on the part of most participants, it is an excellent way to capture everyone's attention and keep them quiet.

I know that being trapped in a moving vehicle for extended periods is not the best situation for building domestic love and harmony. Believe me, I am well acquainted with the unpleasant aspects of family travel. With a twelve-passenger van completely filled with big and little bodies, we have had more than our share of whining, crying, shoving, screaming, fighting, teasing, slurping, chomping, chewing, pinching, pushing, poking, and puking. But with a little creativity, you can turn nearly unbearable situations into productive, memorable moments.

Excursions here and there are necessary in our modern society. Learn to use them to your advantage. Be aware of the captive audience sitting beside you, and capitalize on that forced family time to focus on strengthening relationships.

Think efficiency. Time is money. I think we could all use a little more of both. A little planning and a little scheduling can save hours of time and many wasted trips. And every trip saved is spare change in your pocket.

## ☆ SPENDING

I recently came across an intriguing article. It told of a couple who had just completed another in a series of ongoing garage sales—"sorting through their stuff, pricing it, getting up at the crack of dawn, sitting for hours to sell what they could, then packing up the leftovers and restowing them."[7] When it was all over, the wife came to a life-altering awareness. "I realized how much I hated doing that. I decided I didn't ever want to have another garage sale. And it dawned on me—if I quit acquiring stuff, I won't need to sell it."[8]

The family began spending less time on frivolous consumer purchases and more time on meaningful family activities. "They even decided not to have cell phones, cable TV, or the Internet. The result, [the mother] says, is a calmer, more peaceful life. 'We love the freedom living simply gives us. The less stuff you have the less you have to take care of, insure, clean, and maintain. There's just a real sense of freedom.' "[9]

You really don't need the biggest house, the newest car, the nicest clothes, the fanciest furniture, or the most impressive vacation spots. Contrary to what society tells us, bigger and better, and newer and nicer are not prerequisites to happiness. One look at the mixed-up, miserable lives of many of the rich and famous is enough to prove that money and material possessions do not bring peace and purpose to our lives. Happiness comes from living the simple life. It comes from learning to appreciate what you have without always wishing for more.

When feeling pressured to make yet another purchase, ask yourself the following:

1. Am I looking up the economic ladder or down? . . . Who do you use as a standard against which to judge your financial success?

2. How much is my mood impacted by either the lack or the attainment of a physical possession?

3. Do I discard or stop using perfectly good items because they're not the latest style or technology?

4. Do I confuse needs and wants?

5. Do I value and judge people based on material distinctions?[10]

As yesterday's luxuries ever-increasingly become today's necessities, we push our standard of living higher and higher. Let go of pride. It doesn't really matter what the neighbors think or do. There will always be someone who has more than you, and there will always be someone who has less. Don't impulsively or irresponsibly get yourself into situations you cannot afford. Debt is a dreadful, destructive demon that steals serenity and self-respect.

Cleaning up, painting up, and fixing up are certainly worthwhile projects—just don't over do them. Saving starfish need not be an expensive endeavor. Live frugally. Watch for sales, look for deals, clip coupons. Become an enthusiastic bargain shopper. Avoid paying full price. After all, every penny saved at the check-out counter is extra money in your wallet.

Our pioneer ancestors had a motto that seems to have been lost on today's materialistic society: Use it up, wear it out, make it do, or do without. When considering whether to replace something, ask yourself, "Could it be repainted, refinished, remodeled, renewed, or restored?" Sometimes a simple facelift is all that is needed to make something feel new again—and that will be "good enough."

My husband and I have driven used vehicles all of our married life. While our chosen modes of transportation have not always been the latest models, they have managed to get us here and there and back again quite well. By purchasing less expensive vehicles, we have been able to avoid making car payments our entire married life. This has been a tremendous financial blessing.

There are other ways to keep costs down as well. My children have grown up wearing hand-me-downs and thrift store apparel, and contrary to popular assumption, it hasn't stunted their growth or their self-esteem. I have also learned to make bedspreads and curtains to save on the cost of beautifying our home. And most of our furniture has been given to us or purchased at thrift stores or yard sales. With a little effort and creativity, we have turned them into attractive additions to our home. It's amazing what you can do with piece of sandpaper and a can of paint!

Get over the brand-name, designer-label, high-end-store mentality. Discount stores and no-name merchandise are often "good enough." And you can find some very nice things at yard sales and thrift stores—paying pennies on the dollar for items that still have many years in them. Let someone else pay the big bucks initially for that designer label, then you can pick it up secondhand for next to nothing. It is true, in some instances, that you get what you pay for; but you may also be paying a ridiculously high price for that little tag in the back of your shirt that no one ever sees. (Maybe that's why some teenagers wear their shirts inside out—so the label shows!)

Think before you spend. The elusive enjoyment that a new experience, a new dress, a new tool, a new vehicle, or a new piece of furniture provides is fleeting at best; and they are certainly not worth the added strain on the family budget or your marriage if you cannot afford them. The cost of goods sold is not paid in cash only. We need to consider the cost to our spouse, our family, and our overall sense of well-being. The burden of overwhelming financial obligations brings added stress and conflict directly opposed to harmonious living.

Those who participate in prevailing trends

move in a materialistic direction that detracts from their marriages and their relationships. Those who reject them move away from materialism and toward a richer, more relationship-oriented lifestyle. . . .

As you emphasize and value the material, you start to lessen your appreciation for the personal. . . .

Children who grow up in a non-materialistic household . . . enjoy countless advantages. They grow up with a deeper appreciation for the things they have, no matter how modest. They learn to be wise in their spending habits. They develop a strong work ethic. Perhaps most important, they are part of a family that highly values interaction rather than possessions, which in turn fosters a sense of security and belonging. "It is a gift to give a child a sense of where true value is found. The key is to teach them to value something they can find regardless of their financial circumstances."[11]

The acquisition of too many material goods or "keeping up with the Joneses" is costly, burdensome, and time consuming. "Living within your means" means something. After all, if you don't learn to spend less than you make, it will never really matter how much you make because it will never be enough. Sometimes less is actually more. Less junk means more space in the cupboards, the closets, and the garage. Less time shopping allows more time for family or other worth-while pursuits. Less excess and expense means more money in the bank, more financial freedom, and more peace of mind.

## ☆ CHARITABLE DONATIONS

I am convinced that my name has somehow found its way to every charitable list in this vast and varied country. Years ago, I made a small donation to a deserving organization and have continued to make regular contributions to them for more than twenty years. At the time, I had no idea the snowball effect of that one good deed. I have received heart-wrenching letters from every charitable cause you can imagine. Many of these groups send return address labels as part of their strategy to encourage donations. What-ever the occasion—Christmas, Halloween, Thanks-giving, Valentine's, birthdays—I have a label for it. I now have enough labels to last two lifetimes—and they keep coming!

Despite feeling bombarded by too many pleas for help, my heart aches when reading the stories of disease and deprivation and viewing the images of sick and emaciated children from every corner of the world. The hollow, helpless look in their eyes stirs every sensitivity of my soul, and I have often wished for enough money or magic to take away all the pain. Unfortunately, I have neither. While helping others is undoubtedly worth doing, I simply cannot give to all who need my help.

And yet it is my conviction that those who have been blessed with much have an obligation to share with those who are less fortunate. It becomes our privilege and our duty to bless others through generous donations of time and money. These generous contributions, I believe, should not necessarily be given of our abundance but are most meaningful when they involve some measure of personal pain.

> [William Jennings Bryan said,] "The human measure of a human life is its income; the divine measure of a life is its outgo, its overflow—its contribution to the welfare of all." . . . Giving should not begin after you are established and making a robust salary. "If you don't learn to give when you are poor, . . . you will never give when you are rich." . . . "When others suffer, we either look at them and do nothing, or we do something. And if we do something with our finite resources, we will have less. And therein lies compassion."[12]

Even still, our selfless sacrifices will never be able to save every needy starfish that beckons pleadingly from life's seashore. "The interrelatedness of the world links us constantly with more people than our hearts can hold. . . . It is good, I think, for our hearts, our minds, our imaginations to be stretched; but body, nerve, endurance and life-span are not elastic. My life cannot implement in action all the demands of all the people to whom my heart responds."[13] If you give regularly and unselfishly of the abundance of your heart with a yearning to do more, that is "good enough."

## ☆ WORK/CAREERS

The story is told of a successful businessman who asked his young daughter what she wanted to be when she grew up.

"A briefcase," the girl promptly responded.

"Why, sweetheart," her father questioned, "why would you want to be a briefcase?"

"Because then I could always be with you."

> So many business executives take their families for granted only to discover the heartaches of what happens when family takes a backseat to business. . . .
>
> You know deep down what your family means to you. Don't treat it as something that will just take care of itself; it won't. Give it the same attention that you give your working life; the success won't mean much with no one to share it.[14]

Art Williams, founder and president of A.L. Williams and Associates, a multi-million dollar insurance company, outlined his order of priorities:

I believe the right priorities are God first, family second, and business third. You can't just say that; you have to live it.

It always breaks my heart to see people in business who believe that the way to succeed is to put 100 percent of their effort into their business and neglect their family. . . .

Those people may succeed in their business life, but they'll wake up one day to discover that a business is all they have.[15]

If you were to die today, the workplace would go on without you; and, in time, no one at the office would even remember you. It shouldn't be the same at home. Hopefully, your passing would leave a hole in your family that could never be entirely filled and a legacy that would linger for generations to come.

Giving a full day's work for a full day's wage is a worthwhile endeavor. We can even go the extra mile while on the job. We want to be worth the wages we are paid—or more. We want to make our employer glad to have hired us, and we want those with whom we work to regret our resignation or retirement.

But remember, family is what it's all about. We want to make a living that adequately provides for our family's needs and, hopefully, some of their wants. Beyond that, our efforts may be counterproductive.

A high-level business executive visited a small

island in French Polynesia. He wanted to help individuals raise their standard of living and become "successful." He met a man walking toward the ocean and asked, "What do you do?"

The man replied, "Oh, I fish a little, work in the garden a little, and play with my children."

Determined to raise the man's sights to a higher level, the executive asked, "Do you own a fishing boat?"

"Yes, a small one."

"Why don't you sell it and purchase a bigger boat so you can catch more fish? Then you can purchase more boats to catch more fish so you can make more money. After you have a fleet of fishing boats, you can incorporate your business and start spin-off companies to make even more money. As the CEO, you can sell off your companies, put all your money in investments, and retire early."

After working so hard to build his business, the perplexed Polynesian wondered why he would want to retire early.

The executive explained, "So you can fish a little, work in your garden a little, and have time to play with your children."

By the time the fisherman amassed his fortune and retired, his children would be grown. Besides, the executive was suggesting a lengthy, indirect route for accomplishing what the fisherman had already accomplished. Make sure there is purpose in what you do and that your motives are valid.

There are some who *must* work long hours just to make ends meet. May you be blessed with a greater measure of vigor and vitality for your daily toils and with children who understand and appreciate your sacrifice. Be careful, though, that all those extra hours are to provide the necessities and not the niceties. Your family will be better off with more of your time and less of your money. Children *survive* on the tangible but *thrive* on the intangible.

Who you are and what others think of you should not be solely defined by your occupation or your accumulation of worldly wealth. Replacing some of your work time with family time may mean that you will never buy all the things you would like to buy. It may mean the loss of a promotion or a slower climb up the corporate ladder. And it may even mean that you never become the boss, the supervisor, or the president. But if you perform your duties in an honest, conscientious manner, that will be "good enough." And in the end, you will experience a greater overall sense of well-being.

Let us live lives of priority and purpose. If we do not find the proper balance between work and family, our lives will always seem a little off kilter and a little out of focus. Not everything of importance happens at work. In fact, almost none of the truly important or meaningful things happen there.

Saving starfish is an activity that occurs privately and voluntarily far from the office, the factory, or the boardroom. Likewise, many of our greatest achievements will occur in obscure settings far from public compliment or compensation. Life's richest rewards require no reimbursement. People are more important than projects and family is more important than financial victory. If we fail in the most fundamental areas of our lives, nothing we do at work will ever make up for it. As we are poignantly reminded, "No one's dying wish was that they had spent more time at the office."

## ☆ CHILDREN

Parenthood is serious business—probably the most serious, most worthwhile business you will ever do. However, with my older children I think I took it a bit too seriously. I had set nap times and bed times, and I worried intensely if they were interrupted. Every morning we did the teeth-brushing, hair-combing, bed-making routine. And every night, we did it all in reverse. (I wasn't content with simply catching the starfish, I wanted them polished, cleaned, and manicured too!)

I believe that schedules and predictable routines are important for children and parents. They bring order to our lives and cut down tremendously on the chaos and confusion of family life. But we also need to be flexible. Raising children is all about spontaneity and expecting the unexpected.

I am more relaxed these days. Eventually, I discovered that if the baby missed her morning nap, she usually took a longer afternoon nap. Or if she got to bed late one night, she would probably sleep longer the next day. Somehow it all seemed to even out. And, miraculously, I have managed to live through those days when someone is still running around in their pajamas at noon or their hair doesn't get combed. I have also come to the realization that my children's teeth won't all rot out of their head if they miss brushing one time. (I'm just very careful not to mention this around my daughter who is a dental hygienist!)

When my older children were young, I also spent much more time on their attire. I used to plan what they would wear to special events days ahead of time—right down to the hairstyle and ribbons for my daughter and the color of her socks. Purple socks with a pink outfit was unthinkable. Today it is a different story. Today I consider it "good enough" if both socks match each other.

In fact, my children have been known to wear pants with holes in the knees and sneakers with their toes poking out the end. And I have even been guilty of taking my children to public places in clothes that were not clean and hair that is uncombed. I used to wonder about mothers who did that, but now I understand completely.

Sometimes how your children look has nothing to do with lack of finances or fashion. Sometimes it's all about time, energy, and picking your battles. Sometimes getting everyone out the door, in the car, and buckled up is enough of a challenge without worrying about the ketchup from lunch that dribbled down a child's shirt or the toe sticking out of his favorite pair of shoes.

Sometimes there is just too much going on to keep a handle on everything. And children often overlook or neglect certain social norms. More than once I have had to send one of my boys to the bathroom at church to comb his hair before the meeting started. I even had a son try to wear fluorescent green socks to church. Fortunately, I caught him in time.

Another time I was not so lucky. One Sunday as we were all getting settled on the bench at church, I looked over at four-year-old Levi whose short legs were sticking straight out from his little body. There he sat as happy as could be, completely oblivious to the horror coursing through me at the sight of his bright reddish-orange socks hanging out below his dark blue church pants! I leaned over to the little darling and whispered sweetly, "Those red socks really don't match your blue pants. Let's not wear those to church any-more." He nodded agreeably, and I thought the matter was settled.

A few weeks later, however, I noticed his little legs once again poking out from the bench. This time, however, he had one dark blue sock and one bright red sock. I leaned over and said to him (not nearly as sweetly), "I thought we had a talk about those red socks?"

"Oh, I forgot," he responded indifferently.

Even though they were his favorite socks, they somehow never made it back to his drawer after laundry day. That solved the problem.

And yet I have discovered that sometimes the best solution to my children's wardrobe woes is no solution at all. What do you say to your five-year-old when she tromps into the kitchen proudly modeling the outfit she has chosen for herself—the one she got into all by herself—stripes and plaids in colors that don't go together at all and socks that are three sizes too big? The only thing I could say to little Melia was, "Wow, sweetheart, you got dressed all by yourself. What a big girl you are!" At the same time I was thinking, *Do I really have to take you to Cub Scout Pack Night in that outfit?* I really had no choice, so off we went that summer evening—my daughter in mismatched shirt and shorts with the heel of her red and green Christmas socks half way up the back of her leg!

Sometime before her fourth birthday, Marissa fell in love with cowboy boots. She would wear nothing else. When the first pair wore out, she got another pair for her birthday in February. She wore them everywhere. When summer came, she still insisted on wearing them—even with shorts—and I could not convince her to change them even when we went out in public.

There was a time when I would have been horrified to take my child out in such a ridiculous ensemble, but not anymore. Fighting with a four-year-old over her outfit was a battle I knew I would never win, and it wasn't worth trying. Besides, all the essential parts were covered; and she thought she looked magnificent. I know now that some things can't be helped—and that sometimes "good enough" is good enough.

This is true of teenagers as well. We can spend our time nagging teenagers about their pants that are too long or too short, too tight or too loose; the length and style and color of their hair; their makeup; their shoes; their jewelry; and their multiple piercings that we fail to notice anything good about them. Often these outrageous styles are merely passing fads that the teen will eventually come to recognize as bizarre and foolish if no one is constantly drawing attention to them. In fact, they are often a teen's way of getting noticed. Perhaps if we noticed other more important things about them, they would not have to take such drastic measures to get our attention.

Years ago, one of our sons decided to let his hair grow out a bit. With naturally curly hair, it wasn't long before he had quite a bush on top of his head. Despite our repeated coaxing, he refused to cut it.

One day while relatives were visiting, they commented on his new hairdo. My husband and I rolled our eyes helplessly, making some sarcastic comment about teenagers.

However, my husband's aunt responded rather nonchalantly, "As long as it's not illegal or immoral, don't worry about it." Surprised by such a casual comment by one whom I viewed to be very conservative, I reflected on her statement again and again. With the passing of time and an increased number of teenagers at the Bowen home, I have come to appreciate the wisdom of her words.

Parents, pick your battles carefully. Not every issue with your teenager requires a major assault. Allow your children to show their independence in unimportant areas, and be willing to ignore some things for the greater good that will be achieved in the long run. As long as it is not illegal, immoral, or unethical, let them learn from their own mistakes. Experience can be a most effective teacher. Most teens will eventually get over this peculiar stage of life and, believe it or not, turn out to be responsible, reasonable members of society. (After all, you did!) In fact, they will turn out so well that they will, in your most unbiased opinion, end up raising the most wonderful grandchildren this world has ever seen.

I have also learned another important principle about children: A little bit goes a long way. A few minutes coloring, exploring their hut, riding bikes, reading stories, playing catch, or letting them drive the car can make all the difference—and is often "good enough." Everything seems larger and longer to children. In their young minds those few minutes spent with them here and there grow into something much more as time goes by.

Before my ninth child was born, I started playing a game of tag with my little boys who were still at home. It involved a lot of running and chasing and tickling; and they loved it. However, I didn't feel much like running while expecting the baby or for some time thereafter. Then we moved, and there was much packing and unpacking to be done; and then there was another baby. Once again, I didn't feel much like running. Several years passed without playing our game, and one day Abram lamented aloud, "We always used to play that game." In truth, we had only played it a handful of times, but in his little-boy mind that memory occupied a very large spot.

While spending time with children is absolutely worth doing, you do not need to feel obligated to spend all day with them. Children can be very demanding little people. My children would be thrilled to have me spend all day playing with them, reading to them, or watching them play, but in my grown-up world, that is not possible.

A few minutes watching the spider crawling up its

web, inspecting the bird nest in the apple tree, or pushing them in the swing are precious and memorable; but children must also understand about appointments, meetings, and schedules and the many obligations of our adult lives. They must understand that while they are definitely a priority, we cannot always spend as much time with them as we or they would like.

Tell them you will read two stories to them and then you must fix dinner or do the laundry. Or tell them you will push them in the swing for twenty minutes then you have to clean house. Even better, involve them in your activities. This will allow you to spend more time together, while simultaneously getting the work done. Furthermore, your children will feel important and grown up as they help with your adult tasks.

Raising children doesn't have to be as hard as we sometimes make it out to be. It is easy to come unglued and overreact to some of the quirky things our children do. Step back a moment and ask yourself, "Does it really matter?" Thankfully, our children will eventually outgrow most of their absurd antics and fantastic fads. A little more patience, a little more tolerance, a little more flexibility will go far in getting us through these growing-up years. Childhood does not last forever—even though some days it seems like an eternity. Spend more time loving, enjoying, and appreciating, and less time worrying, harping, and criticizing.

## ☆ EDUCATION

Einstein is synonymous with genius. However, as a child, Albert Einstein's parents "were concerned that he scarcely talked until the age of three."[16] And, while he "got generally good grades . . . Einstein hated the academic high school he was sent to in Munich, where success depended on memorization and obedience to arbitrary authority."[17] Consequently, most of his learning occurred at home. One of his teachers finally suggested that he leave school because "his very presence destroyed the other students' respect for the teacher."[18] He took the teacher's advice and spent the next several months "wandering and loafing."[19] Eventually he graduated from the Federal Institute of Technology in Zurich—"working hard in the laboratory but skipping lectures, [and] graduated with an unexceptional record."[20]

Similarly, Thomas Edison had only three months of formal education. While in school he was a poor student because his mind had a tendency to wander. Furious when the schoolmaster called him "addled," his mother immediately took young Thomas out of school and began homeschooling him. Of this experience, Edison declared, "My mother was the making of me. She was so true, so sure of me, and I felt I had some one to live for, someone I must not disappoint."[21] Edison went on to become one of the world's greatest inventors with 1,093 U.S. patents and many more in the United Kingdom, France, and Germany.

Academic excellence is a worthy goal, but we must remember that grades aren't everything. Grades are only very artificial barometers for measuring a child's progress, and they do not tell the whole story. Some children do well in school because they like to learn or want to please their parents or the teacher. Others have learned to manipulate the system. Some children do poorly because they are slow or shy. Others don't test well or have a different learning style than that practiced in public schools. Just because a child does not progress at the same pace as other children is not necessarily cause for alarm.

Those who rise to the top of their class definitely have an advantage. They are eligible for more scholarships, have more career options, and can be more selective about which colleges or universities they attend. Excelling in school and getting as much education as possible definitely give our children a head start on life. But, as we learned from the tortoise and the hare, having a head start does not determine how the race will end.

Not all of our children will attend Ivy League schools and not all of our children will become doctors or lawyers—nor should we want them to. Who would be left to run the banks, manage the stores, build the houses, fly the planes, grow the crops, and teach the next generation of children? Our children can acquire an excellent education at the local college or technical school and still make a meaningful contribution to society. And there are numerous ways of making a living without ever attending an institution of higher learning.

Unrealistic expectations create undue pressures on children, which leave them feeling inferior and inadequate. They can also create unnecessary stress and worry which manifest themselves in a variety of physical ailments. Fear of punishment or of disappointing parents can also lead children to take drastic measures such as lying and cheating their way through school. Children should not have to sacrifice their honor or their self worth for an arbitrary grade on a little piece of paper.

Even within families there can be great disparity between the academic skills of siblings. Just because Johnny makes the honor roll every quarter doesn't mean his brother Jimmy will too. Each child is blessed with different strengths and abilities, and we need to be careful about having the same expectations of each child. Certainly we can assist, prod, persuade, encourage, support, inspire, cajole, and motivate; but we must not force, demand, bully, compel, coerce, threaten, intimidate, or humiliate. There is a delicate balance between promoting laziness and apathy and pushing a child beyond his capacity. Be wise in your expectations.

Keep in mind that most of our children are just average, ordinary children. If your child exceeds average and consistently earns "A" grades, good for him. If not, the chances are still extremely high that he will lead a happy, productive life.

Also keep in mind that some of what takes place in school is just busy work. Trivial assignments consume too many precious hours of our children's time. I prefer that my children focus on the basics of reading, writing, and arithmetic; and I have dedicated a significant portion of my life ensuring that they succeed in these areas. I do not, however, insist that they spend a lot of time perfecting tangential, less meaningful coursework. In fact, the rebellious side of me is often tempted to tell them not to even bother with those assignments at all. Still, we understand there are certain hoops they must jump through in order to survive the system; and, gratefully, my children's internal initiative has propelled them forward when the class or the curriculum seems unwarranted or wearisome.

My sister once spent several days sitting at the computer with her daughter, helping her complete a very tedious school assignment. When at last complete, they proudly carried it to the teacher for some much-needed validation of their monumental effort. The teacher quickly scanned through the pages of the assignment, made a mark in her book that it had been completed, and unceremoniously set it aside. The magnitude of the project demanded more than a casual and superficial review, and my sister was furious—and rightly so. Her daughter was devastated. Why had the teacher given such a time-consuming assignment if she had only intended to give it a cursory glance? This was definitely a time when "good enough" would have been good enough.

In my seventh grade history class, I was given the assignment to write a three-page report. My father, who was a school teacher by profession, suggested that I put a random thought in the paper to see if the teacher actually read it. So, in the middle of the paper I wrote, "If you read this, I'll buy you a candy bar." I received high marks on the paper . . . and the teacher never said a word about the candy bar!

Finding a strategy for successfully maneuvering through the public school system can be tricky business. There are definitely some classes and assignments that deserve our very best effort, and there are definitely times when getting good grades or excelling on a test may be crucial. But there are also classes and assignments that our children can get through with minimal effort. Learn to distinguish between the two.

Back off. Ease up. Good grades do not automatically ensure success any more than flunking out of school means flunking out of life.

My own father was a high school dropout. Later

he returned to school and eventually completed a Masters degree. He has lived a productive, successful life despite the doubts some may have had of him when he decided he was through with school at only fourteen.

The president of Yale University once passed on some great advice to another college president: "Always be kind to your A and B students. . . . Someday one of them will return to your campus as a good professor. And also be kind to your C students. Someday one of them will return and build you a $2 million science laboratory."[22]

Who a child is or what he can become is not decided by the teacher, the school, or that flimsy slip of paper that comes in the mail at the end of each quarter. Many of the Einsteins and Edisons of the world have found success in spite of their lack of formal education. Not all learning occurs in the classroom. Saving starfish, after all, does not happen while sitting at a desk in a room full of students. Some of life's greatest lessons are learned while quietly traversing the lonely beaches of life. Perhaps the most profound lessons of life are learned in the school of hard knocks, and the final report card for each of us is still waiting to be written.

## ☆ EXTRACURRICULAR ACTIVITIES

Whenever I drive by a school or a park on a stormy Saturday morning and notice the throngs of parents huddled under blankets and umbrellas, watching their children run up and down the field in the rain, I wonder to myself, *Is anyone really having fun?* I suppose it is entirely possible that someone out there loves that cold, miserable, drowned-rat feeling. Then again, maybe all those parents do it because all the other parents do. And just maybe . . . all those other parents don't like it either!

I have a confession to make. With ten children, I have only had one son play soccer one season. There may be some who think that borders on child abuse. But despite my children's maltreatment, they have miraculously managed to grow into happy, well-adjusted, successful people—without ever being on a soccer field! In no way am I being critical of children who play soccer or their parents who watch them play. I am simply trying to make a point: You are not being a bad parent when you scale back your children's activities, and they will not grow up disadvantaged. Like starfish on the beach, there are numerous worthwhile activities for our children, but they cannot do them all. Too much of a good thing can actually be a bad thing.

In today's world, there is a tendency to focus on the needs of the child at the expense of the family. This produces self-absorbed, insensitive children who grow up disrespecting themselves and their parents. We do our children a great disservice by allowing the focus of their lives to be so lop-sided.

Furthermore, if everyone is so busy with extra-curricular activities, who does the chores around the house and when do they get done? Are your children learning what it takes to run a household? Will they be prepared for the time when they must care for themselves and their future families? At no other time in our children's lives will the focus on oneself be so out of balance.

Does little Sally really need to be in five dance and gymnastics classes? Or does robust Johnny need to go out for every sport your town or high school offers? Do you feel pressured to involve your children in activities because all your neighbors or extended family members are doing it? Can you really afford to have your children do everything they want to do?

> The amount of children-and-parent time absorbed in the good activities of private lessons, team sports, and other school and club activities . . . needs to be carefully regulated. Otherwise, children will be overscheduled, and parents will be frazzled and frustrated. Parents should act to preserve time for family prayer, family scripture study . . . and other precious togetherness and individual one-on-one time that bind a family together and fixes children's values on things of eternal worth.

Family experts have warned against what they call "the overscheduling of children. . . . Among many measures of this disturbing trend are the reports that structured sports time has doubled, but children's free time has declined by 12 hours per week, and unstructured outdoor activities have fallen by 50 percent. . . .

Team sports and technology toys like video games and the Internet are already winning away the time of our children and youth. . . . Some young men and women are skipping Church . . . or cutting family time in order to participate in soccer leagues or to pursue various entertainments.

We have to forego some good things in order choose others that are better or best because they . . . strengthen our families.[23]

Whatever happened to children gathering in the neighbor's backyard or the empty lot down the street for a spirited game of baseball, kick the can, or hide and seek? That activity involved no vehicles, no traffic, no money, and no commitment on the part of parents. The children played happily for an hour or two while getting a healthy dose of fresh air and exercise. At the same time, parents got a brief reprieve from the children and a chance to catch up on their work. In the end, everyone came together renewed and ready to face life again. (And when it rained, they all stayed inside!)

Let's be honest. Most of our children are just ordinary kids with ordinary abilities. Most children will not turn out to be concert pianists or college athletes, so why do we insist on acting like they will? With doting parental affections, there is a tendency to overrate our children and, consequently, push them—and ourselves—too hard.

No doubt some children are unusually gifted or talented and a great deal of expense and effort may be justified to help these children reach their full potential; but too many of us, I believe, make extraordinary and unnecessary efforts for our children. For most children, a two-hour trip to the big city for special coaching or training or lessons is really not necessary. Most likely, there is a team or a teacher in your own little community who could do a "good enough" job of helping your child learn whatever it is they want to learn. If you can't find a teacher, maybe your child really doesn't need to learn it.

Is it something they could do without? Are you doing this for the child or to fulfill an unmet need in yourself? Will their adult life be severely disadvantaged if they do not have this experience? Is it even something that will benefit them as they move on to adulthood? Can you afford it? Is it worth the sacrifice that will be made by you, the child, and the rest of the family? Does little Sally even like to dance? Does Johnny really want to play baseball? These are all questions we should seriously consider before committing ourselves and our children to something that will further complicate our already hurried and hectic lives.

Many parents spend a high percentage of their children's growing up years hauling their precious cargo here and there and back and forth. Too often these parents become full-time taxi drivers and part-time parents. Literally living in the fast lane, many mothers have mastered the art of propping bottles for the baby in the car seat and quizzing children on spelling words while dodging in and out of traffic. These parents are short on time, low on energy, high on stress, and out of patience as evening after evening and most Saturdays are filled with one activity or another. Pulled in too many directions, families don't have time to connect and get reacquainted.

In truth, I think it would be much to our children's advantage to be involved in fewer extracurricular activities, thus allowing more time to enjoy their childhood and their families. I think there is much to be said for the good ol' days when Father read the newspaper while the children played happily beside him. Later that night, after cleaning up the kitchen following the evening meal, the family sat together on the sofa listening to the latest radio program—and that was "good enough" for everyone. The focus of the family was more on unity and togetherness and less on individuality and separation.

Call me old-fashioned, but I love having the family gather around the dinner table in the evening as we enjoy a meal together. With a large family, there is always a fair amount of elbow bumping, knee knocking, chair rocking, and milk spilling that goes on. But there is also a lot of joke telling, advice giving, event sharing, and family mingling that accompanies the meal. I also enjoy being together after the meal—cleaning up, laughing, talking, reading stories, and playing games. It is surprising what you can learn about each other and the camaraderie that develops between parent and child and among siblings when you aren't distracted by television, the computer, or other activities. "Parents may be undervaluing themselves when they conclude that sending kids off to every conceivable extracurricular activity is a better use of time than an hour spent around a table, just talking to Mom and Dad."[24]

Please do not misunderstand. In no way am I saying that children should never participate in extracurricular activities. I have had children involved in soccer (one son, one year), basketball, wrestling, track, dance, and a variety of academic activities. Additionally, all of my children have taken piano lessons a minimum of five years—some much longer. However, all of my children have not been involved in all of these activities at the same time. And, except for piano lessons, they have not participated in these activities year after year.

I am careful and selective about the activities my children participate in because I realize they will directly impact me and, consequently, the entire family. Often my children have been involved in activities that were close enough that they could walk or ride their bicycles. Sometimes we carpooled with a neighbor. And I must confess, I have not made it to every game or meet, but I have been to "enough" that the children know that I care and am interested in what they are doing. I hope they understand about the times I am not there. Until cloning becomes a viable option for being in two places at one time, I must make choices. I cannot be all things to all people at all times. Crazy is not a good way to live life.

Years ago my husband took up bagpipe playing. He loved the music. However, the bagpipes are not an instrument that can be played leisurely. They require daily practice to keep up the lung capacity necessary to play the instrument. And they are not an instrument that can be played in the house—at least not pleasantly. Furthermore, the real joy of bagpipe playing comes from being part of a marching band.

After one summer of running here and there to various parades—me sitting on the sidelines with two little children and a third on the way—we decided this was not a family-friendly hobby. Instead of bringing us together, this activity was pulling us apart; and we decided it wasn't worth it. The bagpipes were eventually sold in order to purchase a piano that all the children could learn to play.

The decision was made after much careful consideration and significant sacrifice on my husband's part. We reasoned that one piano would do for all the children, and it was an instrument that would benefit them their entire lives. An added benefit of having all the children involved in the same instrument is that we were spared the painful prospect of sitting through even more music recitals! For our family, that has been "good enough."

Making choices and eliminating activities is more easily accomplished when we recognize what we gain as a family in exchange for what we are giving up. "As we consider various choices, we should remember that it is not enough that something is good. Other choices are better, and still others are best."[25]

He who bites off more than he can chew, soon tires of chewing. Life was meant to be enjoyed—one delicious bite after another—not all at once. Don't rush through the buffet line of life so quickly that you fail to appreciate the meal. Select a few items to be savored and enjoyed—then you won't get indigestion.

Weigh your options carefully. When you are stretched too thin, something will eventually snap. Neither you nor your children can do it all. Set limits and be realistic in your undertakings. Too many children are so overscheduled that they miss out on childhood.

Childhood is a once-in-a-lifetime opportunity and is much too precious to be missed. Don't deprive yourself or your children of this wonderful experience.

## ☆ FAMILY TIME

Several years ago we approached the children about spending our family vacation at Disneyland. I expected a thunderous roar of approval at this unanticipated announcement. Instead, we were met with some rather glum faces and suprising silence. The summer before we had gone to Yellowstone National Park—a nine-hour drive—which had been just a little too much for the younger children, especially our eleven-year-old who cannot stand to be locked up, belted in, or constrained in any way. The looming prospect of an even longer drive was just too much for him.

To make matters worse, our oldest son—who had been to Disneyland years before—painted a rather dismal picture. "Basically," he said, "it is a very, *very*, VERY long drive in a crowded, noisy van. Once you *finally* get there, you stand in line in the hot sun for forty-five minutes for a two-minute ride. It ends up being a very long, hot, tiring day." A long drive, long lines, short attention spans, and children and parents who would be short on patience—that killed our proposal!

Instead, we went camping in the local canyon. We spent a week cliff jumping, canoeing, river rafting, fire building, barbecuing, and marshmallow roasting. We did a great many exciting things in the fourteen hours it would have taken us to drive to California. The whole vacation was much less expensive and much less stressful, and I don't think anyone regrets the decision.

Family time need not be expensive or exhausting. (Saving starfish costs nothing and could be a great family event.) Too often there is a tendency to associate fun with funds—the greater the donation, the greater the delight. Nothing could be further from the truth.

After an exciting summer of impressive family trips, including visits to several historic sites, one father asked his teenage son which trip he enjoyed most. The son's answer was rather revealing: "The thing I liked best this summer . . . was the night you and I laid on the lawn and looked at the stars and talked."[26]

A couple times each winter, we turn off all the lights in the house, and the entire family joins in a game of hide and seek in the dark. In those two or three evenings a winter, we create memories that linger in the children's minds all year.

We also like to play sardines—which is essentially hide and seek in reverse: one person hides and everyone else tries to find him. When you do, you join him in his hiding spot. I can't tell you how hilarious it is a have a family as large as ours all crowded in the bathtub, on the top bunkbed, or under the kitchen table—and how hard it is to keep everybody quiet!

Homemade entertainment is often the best kind—a game around the kitchen table or a little running and chasing in the yard. There are enough people in our family to make our own backyard sports teams, and we have enjoyed some wonderful impromptu games on cool summer evenings. Years ago we were having so much fun playing lawn games in the backyard that my friend who lived around the block could hear the ruckus and quizzed me about it later. We have also had many fascinating adventures traveling through space and time while reading books as a family. In fact, some of our more memorable family experiences have occurred right at home—spontaneously and accidentally—and free of charge.

In addition to these serendipitous activities, every Monday night at our house is family night. One Monday each month is for games, service, family work projects, or other activities. The remaining Monday nights are reserved for lessons on faith, honesty, kindness, love, and other important virtues. This is, no doubt, a worthwhile endeavor; but I can promise you that not every lesson that is taught is the kind we would be proud to send out over the Internet!

We have had some very nice ones—planned well in advance that involved considerable time and effort; but sometimes when Monday night rolls around, my husband and I look at each other and say, "What are we doing tonight?" One of us will throw something together on the spur of the moment and we call it "good enough." I must confess, sometimes we don't even have refreshments. I know that breaks the first—and most important—rule of family night, but we have done it more than once.

Treats definitely make family night more enjoyable, but they are not essential. Back in the day when there was always a baby at our house, treats—when we had them—often accompanied the evening meal. That way we could use the same fork, cup, and plate and save myself additional clean up later. Besides, later I was usually too busy bathing, feeding, or changing the baby to worry about treats.

The most essential aspect of these family gatherings is consistency. Maintaining that consistency may mean reading a short story or a few verses of scripture and having root beer floats. Maybe it means reading the scriptures without the floats and that is "good enough." By making this family time a habit in spite of the obstacles, it tells the children, "I love you. You are so important to me that I want to spend at least one day a week talking about values and goals and things of eternity." That message is sent week after week—not in lavish lessons and gourmet goodies—but in the predictable routine of simple things.

Small but meaningful rituals like making pizza on Saturday night or having a game night once a week give a sense of stability and predictability to kids' lives. These "non-ritual rituals" may also be the best source of pleasant childhood memories. . . . Research shows that kids predict they will get more joy from recalling simple family traditions than they will from big splashy events like a dream vacation or an expensive present.[27]

"There's no place like home . . . there's no place like home," chanted Dorothy in the Wizard of Oz. I believe she was right, especially if that home is filled with lots of love and laughter. Homemade fun is just what the name suggests—homemade. The homespun fun you create will be unique to your family. It cannot be purchased or duplicated. Nothing is more precious than spending uninterrupted, unrushed quality time with your children. In all the world, there is nothing quite like it.

## ☆ SPIRITUALITY

Striving for spiritual perfection is certainly a worthwhile pursuit, but absolute perfection will never happen in this life; so stop beating yourself up over your shortcomings and past mistakes and failures. Certainly you can set goals for improvement and strive each day to be a little better than the day before. But remember, you need to pass through good to get to best. And when you find yourself temporarily stranded on the "good" plateau, you can still find much of hope and happiness. The scriptures tell us that we will be saved by grace after all we can do. Be willing to accept the wonderful gift of grace in your life, believing that it can make up the difference.

Still, living a gospel-centered life can sometimes be overwhelming. There are a host of responsibilities connected with living the gospel: pray; read the scriptures; attend church; love your neighbor; serve others; visit the sick, the lonely, and the fatherless; fulfill your church callings; spend time with your family. In essence, save every starfish. A lot is expected of us, and at times I find myself saying, "This is too much!"

And maybe we don't need to do it all—at least not today.

> Our Sunday worship and instruction time should not simply leave us with an even longer checklist of things to do. While we know that "faith, if it hath not works, is dead, being alone" (James 2:17), we should also recognize that works without faith are equally sterile. Perhaps we might do less rushing around on Sundays with bulging briefcases, assignment lists, and schedules. Perhaps we could spend more time just sitting, in a sense of perfect stillness, with open scriptures and open hearts.[28]

Slow down. Take time regularly to evaluate the direction of your life and monitor your progress. Little of value is accomplished by aimlessly speeding down the road of life.

In a very practical way, I have come to know that there is a time and a season for all things. While I am raising children there will, of necessity, be some things that will be put on hold until another day. I have also learned to be creative when it comes to gospel living, especially when it comes to finding time for personal things.

During those busy baby years when I literally did not have a minute to spare, I still felt a need for daily personal prayer and scripture study. But how would I find the time? I knew that a few meditative moments in quiet, personal prayer was undoubtedly best; but, quite honestly, it was nothing short of a miracle to have five minutes to myself in the bathroom without someone banging on the door. Sometimes in a crunch I have prayed while feeding the baby, driving the car, or riding my bicycle. At the same time, I also recognize that not all my prayers should be said "on the run."

Even when I do kneel to pray, however, many of those prayers are interrupted by a little one calling for me, climbing on me, or poking at me (the closed eye lids are always a favorite attraction). Still I persist. As annoying as those untimely interruptions sometimes are, I cannot help but wonder about the powerful effect they have had on my children to find their mother on her knees in prayer.

Long ago I figured out a clever technique for caring for babies and reading the scriptures. Often when it was time to feed the baby, I found seclusion in the wooden rocking chair in my bedroom—reading and feeding simultaneously. Later, when the baby moved on to a bottle, I held the baby's head in the crook of my right arm, twisting my hand around in such a way as to feed the baby the bottle with the same arm. With my left hand, I held the scriptures. When it was time to turn the page, I set the book on my lap—or on the baby—turned the page, picked the book up, and continued reading. While admittedly not the most comfortable position, I have read hundreds of pages of scripture in that very manner. In fact, I read the entire Old Testament while feeding and rocking my eighth child.

Additionally, Sunday afternoons have typically been a good time to catch up on the week's events by writing in my journal. However, as some of our older children have begun to leave home, I often spend Sunday afternoon typing letters to them. Consequently, the journal writing was getting neglected. One day it occurred to me that with a double click of the print button on my computer, my weekly emails to my children could also be used as journal entries.

Furthermore, every journal entry does not need to be a complete composition. When time is short, a few lines are better than nothing. In that brief synopsis of your week, the reader can glean much about the busyness of your life by reading between the lines.

I once heard someone describe an old journal found in a thrift store. It was the diary of a farmer from a by-gone era. Day after day, the busy farmer made the same entry: "Done chores." While it would have been nice for him to have elaborated about the specific duties performed, those two little words carry a profoundly insightful message. In a straightforward yet powerful way, we learn volumes about the persistent, on-going steadiness of this man's life. You can do the same as you record your personal comings and goings.

Ease up. Even as important as the spiritual side of life is, it still requires a healthy dose of realism. It isn't healthy to run faster than you have strength.

Sometimes when we hear a talk in church on genealogy or family history work, my husband will come home feeling a bit discouraged. "Don't you feel guilty for not doing genealogy?" he will ask.

*"No, I don't!"* I reply emphatically. "I try to write in my journal once a week—that is family history. I am working on getting all the photographs in albums where they can be easily accessed—that is family history. I have a file for each of the children where I put

little snips of their first haircut, their first tooth, and all their special papers from church and school—that is family history. My older children have even taken it upon themselves to do their own scrapbooks; and someday when life slows down a bit, I may get around to helping them. For now, that will just have to be 'good enough.' "

I applaud those who have time to work on genealogy. I think it would be a wonderfully rewarding activity. Someday I hope that I too will have time to work on it. At this point in my life, however, I refuse to feel guilty over the fact that I have not traced a single line all the way back to Adam!

In addition to filling my own spiritual reservoirs, I am also responsible for helping my children find spiritual strength and success. My church has programs for the children and youth to help them become more well-rounded individuals, establish positive priorities, and develop habits that will bless their lives as they move into adulthood. The program for children is called Faith in God, the program for young men is called Duty to God, and the program for young women is called Personal Progress.

A few years ago, my husband and I attended a meeting where the Young Men leaders were emphasizing the benefits of the Duty to God program in the lives of our teenage sons and the important role parents played in helping them achieve this award.

Their leaders did an excellent job of encouraging and motivating the parents in attendance. As the meeting wore on, however, I found myself becoming increasingly disturbed. In fact, I was so discouraged that I went home from that meeting in tears.

As I sat there during the meeting, I felt a crushing burden bearing down on me. Despairingly, I brooded, *I have five sons who still need to earn this award. Those same five sons also need to become Eagle Scouts. Three of those five sons still need to earn their Faith in God and their Cub Scout Arrow of Light awards. PLUS, I have two little girls who need to earn their Faith in God Awards and three daughters who need to earn their Personal Progress Medallion.*

"I can't do it all," I sobbed to my husband through my tears when we returned home. "This is too much for one mother."

I felt so overwhelmed by the enormity of it all that I wanted to quit before I had even started. However, as I thought about it during the following week, one idea kept coming to me, "The best way to eat an elephant is one bite at a time." Eventually, I came to the realization that my children did not need to earn all of these awards that week, that month, or even that year. These projects would be more manageable if I broke them into bite-sized pieces. At length I came up with a workable plan: if each of the children passed off one or two requirements every Sunday, we would eventually—bite by bite—eat this elephant.

It also occurred to me that salvation was not based on becoming an Eagle Scout or earning a Duty to God award or a Young Women's Medallion. If some of my children did not receive some of these honors, it would still be all right. We need to be careful about confusing the essentials of salvation with the non-essentials.

Furthermore, when it comes to gospel living, what may be "good enough" for me, may not be good enough for you. The reverse is also true. You cannot use your neighbor, friend, mother, father, brother, sister, aunt, or uncle as a barometer for your own spiritual well-being. Do not make the mistake of comparing yourself to others. We each have different life situations and different capacities, and God has different expectations for each of us. The best barometer for how well you are living the gospel is the Spirit. If it is nagging at you to do more, you probably need to do more. Be certain, though, it is the spirit nagging at you and not your own internal drive or outside peer pressure causing unnecessary stress.

Learn to distinguish " 'between divine discontent and the devil's dissonance.' The Savior invites improvement to encourage us in reaching our potential. The adversary deploys derision to discourage us with feelings of worthlessness."[29]

The gospel is a plan of happiness. Keep it simple.

"Life is to be enjoyed not just endured."[30] It is possible to maintain eternal priorities and perspective while enduring earthly perplexities.

Christ taught a powerful lesson on priorities and keeping things simple when he visited Mary and Martha at their home in Bethany. You remember the story. Martha was busy making all the necessary dinner preparations. I am sure she put out her very best tablecloth and dishes. Perhaps she even picked some wildflowers from the hillside to set on the table. And, no doubt, she had planned a wonderful menu.

In Luke 10:40–42 it says:

> But Martha was cumbered about much serving, and came to him, and said, Lord, dost thou not care that my sister hath left me to serve alone? bid her therefore that she help me.
>
> And Jesus answered and said unto her, Martha, Martha, thou art careful and troubled about many things:
>
> But one thing is needful: and Mary hath chosen that good part, which shall not be taken away from her.

Certainly, preparing a meal for Christ was worth doing. I know if He came to my house for dinner, I would be busy checking the tablecloth for stains, setting out the very best dishes, and fixing a feast fit for a king. But Christ lovingly and gently taught Martha that all of the fussing and fretting was not the most important thing—even for Him. Instead, it was Mary who had chosen "that good part" when she fell at His feet, feasting on His every word.

My basic nature is more like Martha's. Since becoming a mother, however, I have learned that I cannot do it all. Moreover, I have learned that not all things are of equal worth or merit equal attention. On a daily basis, there are choices to be made on how I will spend my time and what will be my greatest priorities. Sometimes that involves incredible internal turmoil because I really do want to make those cute handouts for my presentation, the new decorations for the Christmas tree, and the matching pajamas for everyone in the family. I have learned over the years, though, that some things really don't matter, and I have learned to let some things go. By striving to be a little less like Martha and a little more like Mary, I have found greater spiritual peace.

## NOTES

1. Calvin Trillin, "Body, Mind, and Soul," *Educators Mutual* 27, no. 5 (May 2007): 8.

2. Nancy Gibbs, "The Magic of the Family Meal," *Time* in partnership with CNN, June 4, 2006, http://www.time.com/time/printout/0,8816,1200760. html.

3. Dallin H. Oaks, "Good, Better, Best," *Ensign,* Nov. 2007, 106.

4. Eric Abrahamson and David H. Freedman, *A Perfect Mess: The Hidden Benefits of Disorder* (New York: Little, Brown and Company, 2007), 7.

5. Ibid., 133.

6. David H. Freedman, *A Perfect Mess: The Hidden Benefits of Disorder,* quoted in *Educators Mutual* 27, no. 7 (July 2007): 6.

7. M. Sue Bergin, "Enjoying a Richer Life," *BYU Magazine* (Winter 2008): 18.

8. Ibid.

9. Ibid.

10. Ibid., 19.

11. Ibid., 18–19.

12. Riley M. Lorimer, "Solid Financial Future," *BYU Magazine* (Winter 2008): 37.

13. Anne Morrow Lindbergh, *Gift from the Sea,* 118.

14. Arthur L. Williams, Jr., *All You Can Do is All You Can Do, but All You Can Do is Enough* (Nashville, TN: Oliver-Nelson Books, 1988), 202.

15. Ibid., 202.

16. "Albert Einstein in Brief," American Institute of Physics, http://www.aip.org/history/einstein/inbrief.htm.

17. "Formative Years," American Institute of Physics, http://www.aip.org/history/einstein/early1.htm.

18. Ibid.

19. "Albert Einstein in Brief," American Institute of Physics, http://www.aip.org/history/einstein/inbrief.htm.

20. Ibid.

21. Mary Bellis, "The Life of Thomas Edison," http://inventors.about.com/od/estartinventors/a/Thomas_Edison.htm.

22. Arthur L. Williams, Jr., *All You Can Do is All You Can Do, but All You Can Do is Enough, Oliver-Nelson Books,* 171.

23. Dallin H. Oaks, "Good, Better, Best," 105, 107.

24. Nancy Gibbs, "The Magic of the Family Meal," *Time* in partnership with CNN, June 4, 2006, http://www.time.com/time/printout/0,8816,1200760. html.

25. Dallin H. Oaks, "Good, Better, Best," *Ensign,* Nov. 2007, 104, 105.

26. Ibid.

27. "Creating Happy Memories," *Educators Mutual* 27, no. 12 (December 2007): 6, quoting Ellen Galinsky of the Families and Work Institute.

28. David S. Baxter, "Overcoming Feelings of Inadequacy," *Ensign,* Aug. 2007, 14.

29. Ibid., 13.

30. Gordon B. Hinckley, "Stand True and Faithful," *Ensign,* May 1996, 95.

# You Cannot Save Every Starfish

Early one morning, a young man was walking down a lonely beach when he saw an old man in the distance throwing something into the sea. As the young man approached, he watched the old man pick up a stranded starfish and throw it into the water. Again and again, the old man kept throwing starfish.

"What are you doing?" asked the young man. The old man explained that the starfish would die if left on the beach under the morning sun.

"But there are thousands here on the beach!" cried the young man. "You can't possibly save all of them—you can't even make a difference!"

The old man looked at the starfish in his hand and then threw it into the safety of the sea. Turning to the young man, he said, "I made a difference to that one."[1]

☆    ☆    ☆

And so we conclude where we began—walking barefoot in the sand alongside an old man, who is making a difference one starfish at a time. Again and again, the old man continued even though his contribution was neither stunning nor spectacular. There were no elaborately-decorated tables exhibiting a wide assortment of delectable dishes to celebrate the occasion. No orchestra played soft background music while he performed his service. There were no brightly-colored banners or dazzling displays in honor of the occasion. And no cheering crowds encouraged him onward. He was just one solitary figure strolling softly on the beach, quietly performing an important task to benefit another.

In fact, to his only critic, the task was not even done well. There would still be thousands of stranded starfish when the sun came up. The task seemed like an effort in futility, but still he persisted. In an unheralded, unremarkable way he made his modest contribution to society. Because he wasn't worried about receiving approval or applause, he could be content with the job he was doing. Saving starfish was definitely a worthwhile endeavor, but it could not be done well—not if it meant saving every one.

There is no shame or guilt in not doing it all. Often it is in the undoing or not doing that we find strength to continue doing what we must do. Too many demands is a recipe for disaster. It is in the empty spaces of our lives that we find inner peace and perspective.

Anne Morrow Lindbergh reflects on her experience with collecting and discarding:

> How greedily I collected. My pockets bulged with wet shells, the damp sand clinging to their crevices. The beach was covered with beautiful shells and I could not let one go by unnoticed. . . . But after all the pockets were stretched and damp, and the bookcase shelves filled and the window ledges covered, I began to drop my acquisitiveness. I began to discard from my possessions, to select.
>
> One cannot collect all the beautiful shells on the beach. One can collect only a few, and they are more beautiful if they are few. . . .
>
> For it is only framed in space that beauty blooms. Only in space are events and objects and people unique and significant—and therefore beautiful. . . .
>
> My life . . . lacks this quality of . . . beauty, because there is so little empty space. The space is scribbled on; the time has been filled. There are so few empty pages in my engagement pad, or empty hours in the day, or empty rooms in my life in which to stand alone and find myself. Too many activities, and people, and things.[2]

Likewise, you will never be able to collect all the shells or save all the starfish on the sandy beaches of your life. You simply cannot be all things to all people at all times, but that doesn't mean you can't be something to someone some of the time. Helen Keller observed, "I am only one, but I am still one. I cannot do everything, but still I can do something."[3]

Interestingly, the average honeybee only produces one-twelfth teaspoon of honey during its lifetime.[4] That is such a minuscule amount as to seem hardly worth the effort; but when combined with the efforts of thousands of other bees, something wonderful is produced. Thank goodness honeybees persevere despite the seeming insignificance of what they do.

Similarly, your small, seemingly insignificant contributions do make a difference. Much that is accomplished in this world is done in ordinary ways by ordinary people living ordinary lives. What you do does matter—even the simple, routine, predictable things that are done quietly and without fanfare in the solitude of your private life.

It has been said, "There will always be a conflict between 'good' and 'good enough.' "[5] Sometimes "good enough" is good enough. That does not mean, however, that you should never do a job well. Obviously, there will be times when you want to go the extra mile on an event or a project. And there will obviously be times when it is justified and worthwhile. Just be careful about which times those are. Not everything you do warrants an all-out effort. Some things are nice but not necessary. Albert Einstein wisely counseled, "Not everything that can be counted counts, and not everything that counts can be counted."[6] Simply put, you will maintain a greater level of sanity if you live more of your life *outside* the fast lane.

Slow down, ease up, cut back. Relax. Have realistic expectations of yourself and others. There is no such thing as super men or super women—stop pretending that there is. Give yourself permission to be human. Be content with the realization that you will never be able to save every starfish. And remember, not everything worth doing is worth doing well—even among the things that do matter. Make a difference in your own little part of the world in your own simple way and quit worrying about trying to change the universe—and that will be "good enough."

### NOTES

1. Inspired by the work of Loren Eiseley; see *The Star Thrower*, 171–73.

2. Anne Morrow Lindbergh, *Gift from the Sea*, 109.

3. Helen Keller, "Helen Keller Quotes," http://www.brainyquote. com/quotes/authors/h/helen_keller.html.

4. "Amazing Honey Facts," Golden Blossom Honey, http:// www.goldenblossomhoney.com/amazingfacts.html.

5. Henry Martyn Leland, "Body, Mind, and Soul," *Educators Mutual* 24, no. 1 (January 2004): 8.

6. Albert Einstein, quoteworld.org, http://www.quoteworld.org/quotes/4161.

.